Parables

From

Big Pond

Parables From Big Pond

Daniel Doucet

Edited by James O. Taylor, Ph.D.

Sydney, Cape Breton

Cover painting by Peter J. Rankin,
Mabou, Cape Breton

Printed by City Printers, Sydney Cape Breton

Solus Publishing
14 Beacon Street
Sydney, Nova Scotia B1P 4S9
902-562-8195 (telephone & facsimile)
E-Mail: poneil@highlander.cbnet.ns.ca

Book and cover design by Pat O'Neil, Sydney.
Cover painting by Peter J. Rankin
Printed and bound in Cape Breton.

Canadian Cataloguing in Publication Data

Doucet, Daniel, 1941 -

         Parables from Big Pond
         ISBN 1-896792-03-0

I.   Title.

PS8557.07874P37 1997   C813'.54   C97-950193-8
PR9199.3.D567P37 1997

This book is dedicated to Beatrice MacNeil's East Bay Ceilidhs, where stories come alive to a tune on the fiddle and a good cup of tea.

Acknowledgements

I would like to thank Barbara Cash, parish secretary who expected one of these stories for her bulletin every Friday at 5 o'clock; Jim MacMullin, Greg MacLeod, Anthony O'Connor, and my mother, Lucy, singer of songs and teller of tales.

Also, Jim Taylor of St. Francis Xavier University, his wife, Effie and his Research Assistant Sean MacEachern, for their selection and editing of stories; publisher Pat O'Neil and the parishioners of Big Pond and Johnstown for whom the stories were written.

Introduction

The stories in this collection were originally published in the Sunday Bulletin of St. Mary's Parish, Big Pond and Sacred Heart Parish, Johnstown, Cape Breton. Narratives such as this belong to a long established Christian literary tradition that goes back as far as the Middle Ages.

Daniel Doucet's narratives are written in a chatty and colloquial style. They are short almost anecdotal explorations that use as their starting point a quotation from the Gospels of Matthew, Mark, Luke and John. Though this present collection does not include a story for each Sunday of the year, the stories included are organized generally according to the Christian Church Calendar.

Quiet in tone and simple in style, Daniel Doucet's "modern day parables" show how the message of the ancient stories is relevant to ordinary people who live ordinary lives. The problems that are examined are familiar ones: the husband who must cope with the death of his wife; the community that must come to terms with the fact that the co-op was on the verge of collapse; a wife's struggle to carry on after she has been deserted by her husband; and perhaps most notably and poignantly, the difficulty of being a priest today and the failure of the church and its clergy to meet the needs of their parishioners. We are given sympathetic but critical vignettes about the priest who is perhaps boring, or who sees everything as never "quite right," or who is only concerned with the "building fund."

But all is far from total gloom. There are as many stories, even in the midst of a depressed economy and an unemployed workforce, that centre on the message of hope and joy. The parable for the Epiphany, for instance, compares three politicians to the three Magi, and concludes with the discovery by the politicians that generalizations about Mi'Kmaq, Acadians and Cape Bretoners are at best spurious. The message typically celebrates a hospitality that centres on tea, biscuits, and fiddle-playing - antidotes for despair and cynicism.

The relevance of Christianity to the predicaments faced by the individuals in these mini-stories—the people who inhabit Daniel Doucet's world—is sometimes difficult to see. The style is simple and direct; the diction is as colloquial as a fireside chat with an elderly couple in a Cape Breton kitchen. Daniel Doucet's vision is one that sees beauty in the minutiae of the routine and the apparently mundane, and experiences joy in the rituals of the church. The voice in these stories is never arrogant or dogmatic; rather, it is quiet and reverent. But it is never one of sickly piety either. Daniel Doucet entreats us to see the humour in the struggle of everyday life. But at the same time he shows us that this struggle is often truly heroic.

Jim Taylor

September, 1997

Six thirty in the morning. He lay staring at the ceiling. He needed another hour's sleep, but he knew he wasn't going to get it. He reached over and pushed a button on the radio to get the local news. He did it against his better judgment because he didn't want to hear any kind of bad news, and the odds were in favour of bad news. There was always bad news on early radio.

He had enough bad news of his own to deal with. That was why he had slept for only two hours. His wife, who had divorced him, had been awarded custody of the children. She was taking them with her to Vancouver where she was going to live with her new boyfriend. She could at least have picked a more merciful time. Three weeks from today would be Christmas Eve. But there was not an ounce of mercy in her. She had used up all her mercy a long time ago. And he had squandered it. She had taken him back each time he had promised to seek help for his drinking and his abusive behaviour. Each time he had broken his promise. Broken his promise, broken the dishes, and broken the furniture. The last time he had broken her nose and she in turn had broken the marriage contract. It was all over.

Cold sober now, he was also a bit chilly. This was supposed to be a heated apartment, but the landlord was a bit on the tight side. His own home had been sold in order to divide the assets. There were no assets. He would be in this apartment, or another one like it, for a long time. Worst of all, he had been laid off, leaving him with days and nights on his hands, nothing to do, and nobody to do it with. If he could have kept his home, at least he would have something to work at. He had gone for help for his drinking and for his violence, but it was difficult to motivate himself now that his family was gone for good. He was angry with himself, and at times his anger threatened to destroy him. He had gone shopping for little Christmas gifts for the kids yesterday, and then in a fit of self-loathing he had thrown all the gifts into the tar pond. Then he lay awake most of the night wondering how he could make it up. This morning he was scheduled for a job interview, but he couldn't imagine anyone wanting to hire him in his present state.

He was right about the radio. He ought not to have turned it on. No cheerful news. The first item dealt with the meeting of Canadian finance ministers. They made his wife sound merciful. This was followed by a report on the high school which was closed indefinitely and might even be torn down because of toxic fungus. Looking up at his own ceiling he wondered if the temperature here was high enough to support fungus. On radio, the school superintendent was saying that the fungus should come as no surprise because the building was thirty years old. Looking up at the ceiling still, he wondered how many buildings in this town were more than thirty years old. Perhaps the whole city would have to be torn down.

Finally there was some good news of sorts. A dying child was being deluged with Christmas gifts from people all over the country. Yes, Virginia, there is a Santa Claus. He wasn't sure, and a pang of fear for the child struck him with the coldness of a blade. He remembered that when he was ten years old, the child next door had been showered with gifts when she was seriously ill. The child had recovered and the other children, himself included, had resented her recovery and made her life miserable for a whole year. Be careful with Santa Claus, Virginia.

He was about to flick off the radio when a voice materialized out of the wilderness. A woman from Mabou was talking about an evening of sharing at her church. People, whether they belonged to her church or not, were invited to come and share something of themselves. They could sing a song, play an instrument, bring a drawing or a painting - any talent, gift or skill to share for that evening with whoever was there. It was just what he had wanted to hear for a long time. He thought he would like to go to his own church for Christmas, perhaps even before Christmas, but he couldn't bring himself to do it. He felt too ashamed. He would be as out of place as Herod at the manger with the Wise Men. But his heart was bursting with the need to give and perhaps he could give it in Mabou. In fact, he was sure he could give it in Mabou. He didn't know what form it would take, what he would share with the others. But he had a week to come up with something and a week was plenty of time to come up with just one gift.

"Mary set out at that time..."
(Luke 1:39-45)

It certainly seemed like an extravagance. Driving off to northern New Brunswick for a housewarming. It was an extravagance because their own house was only half built and was going to remain that way for a while yet. If they stayed home they might at least have the gyproc paid for and the kitchen closed off before Christmas.

She didn't want to think about Christmas right now. The house was a mess and there would never be time to straighten it out. She worried about the possibility of being stranded in New Brunswick and not getting back home for Christmas at all. One good snow storm in northern New Brunswick is all it would take. Her mother would never forgive her if she had to spend Christmas in Cape Breton alone.

In spite of this she was going with a song in her heart and a few songs sung out loud. As usual, her husband was being co-operative. He had been willing to spend the week getting the house ready for Christmas. He was equally willing to drive through uncertain weather to what seemed like the end of the world for a one-night celebration. He sang Christmas carols with her. The children, when they weren't fighting, slept in the back seat.

Her sister wasn't expecting her to do this, but she wanted to do it. It was as important to her as Christmas itself. In fact, it was Christmas for her. It was certainly more important than cleaning her house.

11

Her sister was a special person. She had never had a house of her own. Her husband died when their children were small and she had lived in many different places, none of which had been comfortable. But she had managed to maintain her spirit through it all and her positive attitude had paid off. She looked young and healthy, she had educated herself and found a good job, and now, with the help of her oldest son, was finally moving into a new home of her own.

For the sister from Cape Breton, this made her trip to New Brunswick a joyous one. The drive passed quickly and although they hadn't planned this as a vacation, it began to feel like one. There was something liberating about driving away from everything you were supposed to be doing, feeling sorry for your friends back home who couldn't get away, and watching strangers scurrying about with that all-too-familiar look of panic. They stopped at the mall in Antigonish to pick up a few things, just as a reminder of the stress they were missing.

And because they weren't used to driving long distances this time of year, another surprise greeted them. They got to see the land in a way they had not noticed it before. At rest. The barren fields, the naked trees, the boats tied up and covered on the shore. It made them feel as though they too were at rest. And all along the way they enjoyed the signs of winter - wood piles, skidoos, Christmas decorations, winter berries. By the time they reached their destination they felt more refreshed than tired.

Her sister was overjoyed to see them. They cried, they laughed, and they all talked at the same time. She gave her sister the manger set she had brought as a house warming gift and they set it up. Getting back to Cape Breton was no longer important. It would be a second Christmas if she got there. And her mother was a big girl.

❖

It was only two days after Christmas. He was trying to remember what day it was that the church used to celebrate the Feast of the Slaughter of Innocents. He thought it should be today because there was a slaughter of innocents of sorts going on in his own living room.

His wife and children were in the process of stripping down the tree and all of the Christmas decorations. The decorations had been up since early in December. His wife said that was long enough. She was tired of them. The children's toys were strewn all over the house. People were eating everywhere but at the table, and at all times of the day and night. It was time to get everything out of the way and back to normal. Besides, she was having a New Year's party, and she wanted the house to have a fresh look.

It struck him that this was somewhat of a departure from tradition. Although it had been years since they had left the tree up until the Feast of Epiphany, they had never taken it down before the New Year. Even the year his sister died they had all agreed that community celebration came before private tragedy, and they had gone through their grief with the comfort of familiar symbols. This year they certainly were nipping Christmas, if not in the bud, at least in early bloom.

Down came the old angel. He tried to get a last look at it as it was being wrapped in tissue. Who was going to get the messages through to Joseph and the Wise Men now that the angel was losing its face as well as its voice? Down came the star from the window, and the candles. There was to be nothing left for either Joseph or the Wise Men. They would have to look for guidance elsewhere.

Something was very wrong. The family had all borne the stress of early December, preparing for Christmas with the promise that there would be a pay-off at the end. He had actually not minded the shopping, done a bit at a time, the walk through the woods to get the tree and boughs, teaching the children to make wreaths, listening to their endless recitations of what they wanted for Christmas. All of these things had value, but that value was somehow connected with the enjoyment of the results. And this year that enjoyment, in his opinion, had been far too brief.

They had all wolfed down food, scattered paper around, jumped from one gift to another, and now the enjoyment was being put into cardboard boxes. They had gone to church on Christmas Eve, true enough, and that had been exciting. But perhaps that was the problem. Everything was excitement and that excitement was being put away in boxes before it had time to ripen into appreciation, awe and peace. Even if they went back to church right now, the church decorations would seem out of step and no longer connected with what they were all experiencing at home.

There was definitely something wrong with all of this. And worst of all, it was too late to stop it. He could hardly ask the children to decorate the tree all over again. The tree was on its way out the door and a resisting yet aggressive teenager was on his way in with the vacuum cleaner. Whatever traces the tree had left behind were about to follow it into oblivion.

His oldest daughter cast a hurried look in the direction of the porcelain manger figurines resting on the buffet. His own eye fell on it at the same time, almost as if he had anticipated her movement. Perhaps the angel had tipped him off before its head was shoved into the cardboard box. Whatever it was, he understood its significance. The Wise Men had not even arrived yet and there was no way they were going to be shoved into the box before they arrived. Herod had to be stopped, even if he came in the guise of his own beautiful and well-meaning daughter.

He was surprised that his voice sounded so calm and pleasant. He was even more surpirsed that he didn't lecture her or give her a sermon on the commercialization of Christmas. He heard himself say simply that he was enjoying the manger and would like to keep it out until the Feast of the Wise Men. How long was that, she asked. Not too long he said, just long enough for everyone to get to know them.

When she left the room he rescued a few evergreen branches from the garbage and laid them around the manger.

They were three government people all from different political parties. There was a Conservative, a Liberal, and a New Democrat. What had brought them together was a common goal, like the three MPs who went to Iraq to seek freedom for the Canadian hostages. In this case though the mission was much more low-key and private, although it was not secret. One was from Quebec, one from Saskatchewan, and one from the Northwest Territories. They had been hearing about Cape Breton for a long time, most of it bad – failed industry, unemployment, welfare, and government grants. In spite of that they were curious, because they sensed a certain zest for life there that was strong, and they wanted to see it first hand. Perhaps it would offer them a sense of hope for their own impoverished constituencies.

Since they wanted to avoid "party lines" and window dressing, they had made no contact with either local politicians or tourist personnel. Their information was gathered from people they had talked to, both former Cape Bretoners and others who had spent time there. When they compiled their information it was enough to give them, not so much a total picture of Cape Breton, but a flavour of life there.

Word of their arrival did leak out and a local promotional group quickly invited them to a reception where they were treated to speeches and to a performance by kilted dancers. When pressed about what they were looking for, the visitors' answers seemed vague so no official tour was arranged for

16

them. They were invited to meet with the group at the end of their stay and report on their findings.

The homework and preparation the three had done for their trip paid off. They spent a day with labourers who were building houses for members of their union. It was astonishing how simple it was. People caring for people. "Need, not Greed" was their motto. They visited a Mi'kmaw village where they quickly discovered that the generalizations they had heard about native people did not apply. Here they found a growing people working on many different projects, and a high percentage of young people attending university. A laughing people, a people with hope. They visited an Acadian community with thriving co-ops and a local hospital that was about to be taken over by such a co-op.

Between visits they ate biscuits, drank tea, heard the fiddles and enjoyed the stories. They poured out their admiration and their gratitude and they told them of little groups of people who were very much like them in Quebec, Saskatchewan, and the Northwest Territories. They spoke of their own aspirations, and of how they would feel supported by this new life going on in what was described as a dying area.

They went home without reporting to anyone on their way.

"*Slow down a bit.* That car on the side of the road might be in trouble. Those two guys could be looking for help."

"I don't think they were in that car. They've got backpacks. I think they're just students walking home from the bus."

"Guess you're right. Wait, check your mirror. See the white shirts and neckties. They look like Mormons. They've parked their car and they're walking down that lane. Now isn't that something. Going from door to door peddling religion. And them so young they do look like school kids. Did you ever wonder why they travel in pairs?"

"Safety in numbers, I guess. Most of them are Americans, and I suppose they never know what they're going to run into, going into strange places. The nuns used to travel like that in the old days. But they may just be following the way it was done in the Gospel, you know, when Jesus sent them out two by two."

"I suppose so. Well, they must know something we don't. To be able to get two people going door to door to talk religion. When's the last time a Catholic came to your door to talk religion?"

"Well, they're missionaries. I suppose we're considered mission territory. Maybe our own missionaries do that in South America or Asia or wherever they go."

"I don't think so. Besides, our own missionaries would be too old to do it even if they had a mind to. I don't know if we have any missionaries under the age of sixty. These guys are teenagers. Have they ever been to your house?"

"I don't make a habit of letting anyone into my house to talk religion. Guess it's the way I was brought up. When I was a kid the only ones going around were the Jehovah's Witnesses and everyone seemed to be kind of scared of them, like they were evil or something. My aunt used to scream curses at them. I think I was more frightened than they were. They seemed to take it all in stride. I guess they were used to it. But my aunt's screaming really shook me up. I'm still scared by anything that reminds me of it."

"They don't frighten me, but I'm not too keen on talking about religion, even with people I know. Religion is just something we do or we don't do. It's not something we sit around and talk about. Maybe we should. I've seen the Mormons' ads on television and they're pretty good. They usually show how we could save ourselves a lot of trouble if we talked over things in our families, whether it's about religion or not. I think their religion is a lot about family life. And seeing the way things are going these days, it seems that everybody could learn a lot about that."

"Yeah, I've seen the ads too. Mind you the families they show aren't very much like the families I know. Like they're going off to play tennis together or something. Not many families around New Waterford doing that kind of thing these days. Still there's something to it. You can learn from anything."

"Talk about New Waterford or any of the places where people are out of work and I'll tell you who I'm learning a lot from. The Salvation Army. It must be really hard for them, dealing with the kinds of families both you and I know. More and more demands and less and less money in the pot. I feel sorry for them. It must take a lot of courage to keep going, knowing that things are getting worse instead of better."

"I don't feel sorry for them as much as I feel admiration for them. I guess I sort of envy them. I've thrown my bit of money into the Salvation Army kettle on my way out of the liquor store, and I wonder how they can look happy comparing the amount of money in their kettle with the amount in the liquor store's cash register. Same thing at the mall. You have to hand it to them."

"Our own missionaries used to be like that too, although it was always for people from overseas, people who had less than even our poorest people here, like you see on television. They'd be raising money to dig a well or they'd be collecting old school books for kids who had none. They even used to collect stamps. Never could figure out what they did with the stamps. We were told it was to buy black babies. Not for slaves or anything - maybe it was to buy them from slavery. I wonder what the slave owners did with the stamps?"

"Well, there's so many organizations to give to, it isn't a problem finding a way to help out if you have the notion. I guess it doesn't matter what church is doing it, you either help or you don't. I don't see why we can't all pray the same either."

"You mean you'd like to sing in that black Gospel choir that was on Rita's Christmas show. I doubt it. Although it would probably do you good. I'd be better at that. You'd be better in an evangelical church that could heal you of your fear."

"Thanks but I'll stay where I'm at. Besides, if I was to go

to any other church, I'd want to go to the Presbyterian Church in Loch Lomond. One of the nicest around these parts."

"It's closed most of the year."

"What a shame. And what a shame that I've never attended there."

"Good God, did those two young Mormons start all this?"

He had been born a fisherman.

Like his father and grandfather before him. In fact, he told his grandfather's favourite story as if it were his own. At the age of twelve, his grandfather had gone with his own father to Tancook to get a fishing boat and the two of them had brought her home to Cape Breton under sail. They brought her safely through the fog to harbour every night with only a compass to guide them. When he told his grandfather's story, he could hear every sound, sense every smell, feel every contour. It was the world of sail and diesel, fishgut and rope, tide, moon and salt.

It was with a deep burning pride that he had spoken before the television cameras on the wharf only last year when the local fish plant had been closed.

"The government wants us to diversify," he had said. "Is government going to provide computer jobs for all these fishermen? Even if they could train us to run computers, what would we be computing?"

You'd have to be living in Ottawa to concoct a plan like that - to have fishermen give up their boats for computers. That was his opinion and many people agreed. His comments had attracted national attention.

It was now a year later, the fish plant was running again and the talk of fishermen running computers was history. So why was he sitting here listening to a man offering him an office job? It wasn't a job at a computer desk, but an office job is an office job, with no moon, stars or fishgut. He had to be crazy even to listen to the man.

And yet there was a cold clear logic to what the man was saying. The union needed someone who understood fishing, someone who understood fishermen. Someone who could stand up and say what he meant, and say it clearly, with courage. The fishing industry was still in deep trouble and there would be more closures ahead. If all the fishermen were too busy fishing to get involved in the politics, who was going to look after their interests? The professionals, that was who. In Halifax and Ottawa.

He thought of what he would have to give up, and he thought of the dangers of office work and expense accounts. He felt his heart break. He had felt so proud of himself last year, watching himself on the national news. He had known he was telling the truth and he had told it simply and powerfully. If only he had kept his mouth shut. He saw the schools of fish fade off in the distance, he saw the fog close in over the stars and he heard the seagulls cry as he nodded his head and agreed to meet with a hiring committee.

"And His teaching made a deep impression on them..."

(Mark 1:21-28)

They deserved something better.

They were a group of bright people. Bright and creative. There was always something interesting going on in their community. Activities for the children, evening courses for adults in everything from accounting to flower arranging, and a group who met regularly to make long term plans for job creation in the area. It was a community where people smiled a lot. It was a community where you didn't mind that everyone knew your business because they were all friends.

Except in church. Not that people weren't friends in church. You could tell this by the way they greeted one another during the exchange of peace. People shook hands like they meant it, some younger couples even kissed, and one elderly woman went five pews beyond her own, then waved at the rest of the people. People sang along with the choir with good strong voices.

No, nothing wrong with the people. It was the priest who was out of sync. He wasn't a bad person. He wasn't even cross or cranky. Some people said he was just boring. But that wasn't quite true either. People remembered what he said — probably too much. His sermons always seemed to cast some doubt over what the community was doing. Teenage dances might be okay, but there was always the possibility of drugs. The hospital workers might deserve higher wages, but there might be violence if a strike broke out. General absolution might be practical, but people might cheat if they weren't forced to say their sins out loud.

Nothing was ever wrong, but nothing was ever quite right either. There were a lot of Sunday dinner arguments over what he said. A few people stopped going to church. But generally the parish just lurched on.

Now the priest had gone away on holiday as he often did when the swimming was good in Dundee. The old monk who generally replaced him was sick, so a young Scarborough mission priest on vacation in a neighbouring parish was saying the Sunday Masses.

It also happened that a group of parishioners had joined people from other parishes around the lake in a common cause - to stop foreign draggers from working the lake. It had been a matter of concern for some years now and had suddenly erupted into confrontation. There was a lot of nervous talk in the community as to the rightness or wrongness of this action.

The mission priest addressed the matter from the pulpit. He quoted the Old and the New Testament on stewardship, and the popes on respect for the earth. He told stories of the devastation of the rain forests in Brazil. He did not know what was involved in this particular dispute and whether there was indeed a violation of God's creation. But he fully supported the people in their concern and their determination to do something about it. The cause was more important than the protocol. Political damage could always be repaired, but the lake might not be.

How the confrontation was resolved is another story. But that Sunday was never forgotten. The parishioners continued to shake hands at the exchange of peace. They continued to sing. But when the parish priest returned from Dundee, they began to challenge some of the things he was saying.

She $missed$ the $mountain$, although she had never lived there. She had always lived in her house by the highway, the house that her grandparents had built when they had moved down from the mountain. She had never really forgiven them. She felt cheated of her opportunity to have grown up on the mountain.

That didn't bother her grandparents. They had been happy to get off the mountain and they never regretted their decision. Living on the highway meant getting around in winter like everyone else instead of struggling waist-deep in snow. Living on the highway meant seeing the traffic go by, knowing who went where, being in touch. It meant getting away from the lonliness of the mountain.

She understood her grandparents' reasoning but still she could not forgive them. It was easy for them to leave the mountain because in a sense they could take the mountain down with them. It was part of their experience, part of their lives. No matter where they lived, on the highway half a mile from the mountain or in New York City, they would always be mountain people. But they hadn't valued their way of life enough to pass it on to their children. Or perhaps worse, they hadn't valued their children enough to pass on their way of life.

It was Valentine's Day and she felt like a hopeless romantic for indulging in these thoughts. And yet what was Valentine's Day for if not to indulge in things of the heart? There was a wound in her heart. The cause of that wound, though, was not a man but a missing piece of herself that she yearned for. A passion that had been awakened but never fulfilled. The mountain.

There was indeed something real about the importance of the mountain. It had been the life of her people for several hundred years. There were so many songs sung about the mountain, whether it was this particular mountain or mountains that her people had known in ages long past.

"Come by the hills," her grandfather had sung, "and the cares of tomorrow must wait till this day is done." But neither the cares of tomorrow nor of today would wait when you lived on the highway. Even her grandfather as he sang by the window was worried about his pension cheque arriving tomorrow. She wondered why. He hadn't spent last month's yet. Her French-speaking grandmother, in her old age, had sung a number of songs about mountains. "La bas, sur la montagne, j'ai entendu chante...", "away over on the mountain I have heard singing...". What had her grandmother heard on the mountain? The song of the birds? The song of the wind in the trees? The song of silence? Or perhaps the song of her own heart.

It was too late to go back to live on the mountain. She had her house here on the highway and she could barely afford to keep it let alone have it hauled back into the hills. Besides, she enjoyed her creature comforts and wasn't willing to drag groceries through the snow. She had grown up on broccoli and tomatoes in the wintertime and wasn't willing to go back to a cellar full of turnips. No, she wasn't willing to turn the clock back for the privacy and natural flow of the mountain.

Still, she wanted to sing and no sound would come. So she dressed warmly and set out for the mountain. She was out of breath when she got there and fully aware that she would not enjoy having to make this trip regularly. It was sheltered, though,

27

and she was able to sit on a fallen tree to rest. Only the foundation of the old house was left, not enough for her to picture what the house might have been like except that she could tell it had been small. She reflected that while there might have been a stillness outside, there would have been precious little privacy within. She wondered what it would have been like to be free of outside influences like television and telephone, but to be bound so closely to other people physically.

As she sat she began to hear the sounds of the forest, the wind in the trees, the birds, a squirrel that eventually joined her on the fallen tree. These things belonged to a world outside of her, like Oprah on television or her cousin Anna chattering on the telephone. She took a valentine chocolate from her pocket, took a bite and offered one to the squirrel.

Then she waited, and soon the song moved from her heart to her lips.

"Wild beasts and the angels looked after him..."

(Matthew 4:1-11)

He had known for a long time what he wanted to do. He wanted to build a house, and he wanted to build it himself. He was not a carpenter, and he had never built anything more complicated than a bookcase by himself. But he had helped his brother who was a carpenter build a new house in Ontario when he had been there unemployed. What he had going for him most was a keen interest and a good eye. He had enjoyed working with his brother and had learned a lot. He had studied a lot of books too and had talked to different tradesmen.

The main stumbling block was that he lacked the courage to make a start — to actually get at it. But he knew how to get the courage. He needed at least a whole month of evenings to work out his plans in detail, to iron out all the possible problems. More problems would follow, but he would handle those too if he could start out feeling sure of himself.

The more immediate and practical problem was that he didn't have a quiet place to work at his plans. The place where they were living was small; and even when he had the kids put the television in their bedroom, it still distracted him. And so he put a ban on television for the time that it would take him. The children protested and made more noise than the television, but he remained steadfast.

He set up a table next to the small wood stove in the living room, and there he sat, night after night, chewing pencils and messing up papers. His wife worked nights so he had only an hour each evening before she left for work to discuss the plans with her, along with whatever else needed to be discussed.

What saved him was the fire in the wood stove. It saved him in a strange way, because at the same time that the fire had a calming effect on him, it also raised some strange beasts within him. It brought back memories of a time he barely remembered, when all the houses in the village had depended on wood stoves for both heating and cooking, and when fire determined so much of the activity of the family. Cutting the winter wood and hauling it, sawing it, splitting it, cording it, taking it in, cording it again, moving it to the wood box and finally putting it in the stove.

All this made him feel so removed, so distant from what his own home and family were like, that it frightened him. He was caught in two worlds. The world of his past and the world of his children. His children did not know the world of his past. He had managed to silence the television set for a month, but he knew, of course, that it would come back. The house he was building was as much for them as for him. He knew they would reject the house if it was not exactly like other people's houses. They would probably be ashamed of him if it wasn't. At times he felt incompetent, not only as a carpenter and as a parent, but as a man, as a human being. The flames darted about in the stove, like Satan laughing at his insecurities.

He thought of not making a fire and using an electric heater instead. But he discovered that he was hooked, hypnotized by the fire. He also discovered at the same time that he was being assailed by doubts about himself, that the plans were progressing well. He made a decision to trust the fire and get on with his building.

On the fortieth night, he finished the plans. The children had settled down and were spending a lot of time sitting on the floor around the fire, doing homework or playing games.

❖

He wished she would stay away from the meetings. She ought to sense that people didn't want her there and that it was only politeness that kept them from telling her so. She ought to know that she didn't understand the issues and that she complicated things and got people upset. She ought to know she didn't belong.

It was at times like this that he regretted having accepted the presidency of the local Fishermen's Union. It involved so much work. It was important that the union succeed, because he was a fisherman himself, and as the group's success went, so would his own. He had some ideas about what would work and what would not work. Being president certainly gave him an opportunity to promote his ideas. But besides that, he had a deep feeling of pride in his community, and he was willing to put in a great deal of energy to see his community get ahead. Fishing was important, but being part of the union was more than fishing. If they could make the fishing work, they could make other things work too. The thought of inspiring people in his community, of giving them hope, was what really stirred him.

It was also what made him question whether he wanted to be president of the union. Time and again he realized that a great many of the members, perhaps the majority, did not share his concerns for the greater community. What they wanted was to sell fish at the best price. It was as simple as that. Together they had a better chance of bargaining for higher prices. They expected him to want what they wanted. That's why they had elected him. And the more the economy floundered, the simpler his job as president became. There was no time for frills.

This was where she came in. She was a fisherwoman, not a fisherman. They had already indulged her by letting her join the union, or at least so they thought. They had even done it freely and without any controversy. She hadn't needed the Human Rights Commission to intervene on her behalf. She could call herself a fisherman, a fisherwoman, or whatever she wanted. She enjoyed their respect, mainly because her catches were as respectable as their own. No better, no worse.

As he listened to her now, addressing the meeting, he realized that was exactly how she viewed herself — no better, no worse. They had let her in and she behaved like one who was in. She belonged until she was told she didn't belong, and perhaps even after that.   She knew that she saw some issues differently than the majority and that didn't bother her. It didn't occur to her that she was complicating things, because in her view, "things" were already complicated. Life was complicated and that was that.

The issue under discussion was the supplying of new fish species to foreign markets. She was convinced that with everyone working together the local fish plant could, in time, process the new species, thereby providing work for the many women who were now unemployed. The men weren't at all sure that they could afford the time to work the changes. The buyers could go elsewhere, and there was no evidence that the local fish plant could be competitive, even if the fishermen agreed to subsidize it with lower prices.

The men were not receptive to her idea, and he was distressed because she risked being dismissed out of hand. Most upsetting was his responsibility as chairman to ensure that she be heard. It was a tense situation. He felt sure that some of the men were restraining their anger because she was a woman. Others didn't want to sound sexist. To complicate matters for him even more, he knew that in his heart he wanted to hear no more from her. She was forcing him to help her out or reveal himself as a coward. He wished she would go away.

He was saved at the last minute by a man who spoke up in support of the fisherwoman. With a sigh of relief he was able to bring the meeting around to some form of dialogue, however noisy. Feeling his hair turn grey, he considered taking up golfing when his term as president was up.

Her soul was troubled. She wished she could move to Vancouver, to Paris, or better still to Australia. She wished she had listened to her mother and become a nun. She wished people would leave her alone. She wished her children would run away from home. She wished, she wished, she wished.

Three years ago she had been a mousy little woman suffering from mild bouts of depression. At least the doctor had told her it was mild depression when he had put her on a "mild" anti-depressant. Mild to the doctor, not to her. Certainly not mild for her husband whose activities were greatly curtailed because she didn't want to be alone at any time. Not mild for her children who could not count on her as much for all the looking after and all the cheering up and good times they were used to. Her woman friends who had known her when she was a bundle of energy and smiles were finding it hard too, but they were loyal and promised to see her through this difficult time. In fact, they had resisted the whole idea of medication and, together with her husband, had talked her into seeing a therapist.

That was three years ago. She looked into the mirror and wondered where the mousy little woman had gone. Now her husband was angry at her all the time, her children were out of control and her friends accused her of being selfish and ungrateful. And here she was in the middle of it all, letting it all happen, not trying to stop it. She wasn't depressed any more, but she was afraid.

She had taken their advice meekly, submissively. Since she couldn't make decisions for herself she had followed their suggestion and gone into therapy. In gratitude for their help she had given it everything she had. She had worked harder at it than anything else she had ever worked at in her life. She had allowed herself to feel so much hurt inside that at times she felt her ribs would crack. She had cried buckets of tears. She had allowed herself to see hatred inside that she thought only Adolf Hitler was capable of and coldness worthy only of Margaret Thatcher. Underneath it all she had found warmth, gentleness and even joy. But the warmth and gentleness were tempered with and protected by a new strength that had not been there before.

And that was the problem. Her husband, who had been only too willing to look after her when she didn't have a mind of her own, had problems with her as she became increasingly critical of his childish behaviour. Her kids, who viewed her increasing freedom as an opportunity to experiment themselves, were now eating french fries instead of broccoli and doing poorly in school. Her women friends, whose husbands played pool with her husband, were becoming alarmed. She had gone too far, they said. Perhaps she should quit therapy before it ruined her marriage and threatened their own.

Too late. She turned away from the mirror and sat on the side of her bed. Having chosen health, how do you choose to be sick again? She knew in her heart she would never be depressed again. She decided what she needed to do was to gather her strength for the fearful times ahead.

Most of all he felt tired. Tired in his bones, tired in his muscles, tired in his head. It was the tiredness of old age, and yet he was only forty. It was a tiredness that had suddenly overcome him as if it were here to stay. He sat on the back step and felt the weight of his own body move him down into the earth. It was as if his spirit had finally lost its fight against gravity.

His brother was coming home - home to stay. His father was sending an airline ticket in tomorrow's mail and they were to meet him at the airport.

He had not thought that the old man would go through with it. Not after everything that had been said the night before. Not after his telling the old man how hurt he felt.

It just wasn't fair, and he couldn't see how it could ever be fair. He shouldn't have to share everything that was his with a brother who had never contributed anything to the family home. Not a penny, not a thought, nothing.

No, it wasn't fair. It wasn't fair because this home wasn't really a family home anymore. It was his father's home and his home. His father had no right, apart from the legal right, to open it to anyone else.

His father was wrong in thinking that the home was still his to do with as he pleased. His father was discounting twenty years of service, twenty years of loyalty.

Sitting on the back step, he thought of how it had all happened. Happened was the correct word. It had just happened. It had never been planned this way. His father had never asked him to stay at home and he had never volunteered. His mother's sickness and death had been the event that led to his staying, but it had never been spelled out as such. She had taken sick just as he was finishing university. He had taken a teaching job at home so that he could be near her and help out. His father would never have gotten through it without him.

His younger brother, on the other hand, had gone on to Toronto after high school and had come home only twice to see them. Once on a holiday when his mother was sick, not to look after her, but to sun himself on the beach and drink beer with the boys. The second time was for her funeral. Any trips since had been more sun and more beer.

He wondered if he shouldn't have moved out of there after his mother's funeral and let his father make a fresh start for himself. His father had been so depressed, but perhaps if he had been left to bottom out, he would have picked himself up and made it on his own. Difficult to say, in retrospect. What happened was that he had stayed with his father. There had been a lot of sacrifice involved for him. He tried to keep things the way his mother had, and he did things for his father to make it easier in those very difficult days.

But what he had done at first to give comfort and support later developed into habit and routine. His father took it for granted that things would stay the way they were, and the longer it went on that way, the more difficult it became to change anything. It occurred to him now that if his mother had lived there would have been a great many more changes around the place. She would never have frozen them in time this way.

Now, after twenty years of loyalty to his father's need for steadiness and continuity, the rug was being pulled out from under his feet by this same father. Steadiness and continuity be damned . . . little brother was coming home.

His father had the legal right to welcome the younger brother home. But his father was going to have to go to the airport alone. He had no power to change that. And after that, it was going to be one day at a time. Perhaps they would all change, the three of them. He wasn't putting any bets on it.

She was not looking for sympathy from anyone. She had broken the law, was caught, and expected to pay the penalty. She had been collecting unemployment insurance benefits for six months now, all the while doing housework by the day, collecting cash and not reporting her earnings. Deep in her heart she didn't feel like a criminal. It was hard to live on unemployment insurance at the best of times, and this was not the best of times. It wasn't her fault that her husband had been drinking since he'd been fired, that her daughter needed to have an operation in Halifax, and that their rent had gone up. It wasn't as if she had bought a Mercedes or a mink coat . . . she was putting food on the table, paying the rent, and making payments on the car.

She often wondered what people had done before the days of unemployment insurance. Her mother had lots of stories about what real poverty was like, but none of the stories seemed to help very much. She could ask her husband to leave, but he did seem to be putting forth a genuine effort and she felt that with some encouragement he had a good chance of making it. She could sell the car, but then she wouldn't be able to work again. There was no other place to live, and her daughter's health was a priority. There were just too many priorities.

But even though she didn't feel like a criminal, it wouldn't be very long before she would be one. Her legal aid lawyer advised her to plead guilty. She would have to pay back what she had received illegally, plus a fine. She would be given time to pay but he hadn't figured out how she would, or could, do that. If she couldn't live on two incomes, how could she live on one with monthly deductions? She had made a big mistake and she was in deep trouble.

She didn't have the energy left to worry about her reputation, and yet she knew that it had suffered a severe blow. Although the practice of cheating on unemployment insurance was common enough, it was not common in her family. She had never done anything illegal in her life. Her family was proud and she knew she had let them down. She wasn't sure whether she had let them down most by cheating, by getting caught, or by being poor. Although her mother had stories about the hard times, she had a sense that her mother had turned her back on the hard times and was ashamed of her for being poor.

In the wider community there would be little support for her. Those who were cheating, as she had been, would not come forward. They were either too afraid, or in some cases, unwilling to admit that they had a good thing going. Those who didn't cheat would view her as the enemy. They would view her as just another parasite living off the public tax dollar. They would rationalize that if she didn't have enough to eat, she should have asked them and they would have given her food. If she didn't have money to be with her daughter in Halifax, she should have asked them and they would have given her some. If she could demonstrate that she managed her pogey cheque wisely, they would be willing to listen to her.

In her mind she knew she couldn't meet the requirements. There had been times when she'd been too discouraged to cook and had bought expensive junk food. There had been times when she had given her husband money to drink because she was too tired to argue with him. And she had bought some nice clothes for her daughter to cheer her up.

No, she wouldn't pass the test. She would be punished, not only by the justice system but more harshly and more significantly by the community.

She hoped that when the punishment came, she would be able to bear up. Surely, somewhere, there must be something better for her.

$\mathcal{H}e$ *regretted the thousands* of breakfasts he had eaten in haste. He regretted the breakfasts he had eaten but not seen, and the breakfasts he had not eaten at all. The gallons of coffee he had swallowed on his way out the door or behind the wheel of his car on his way to work. Hurrying to get out and hurrying to get home again. The words not spoken because he was not really awake - useless words about useless things.

There was no reason to hurry home anymore. On her hospital bed his wife had just closed her eyes for the last time. It was not a shock. The vigil had been a long one, and he had been faithful. Family and friends had taken turns with him. On this last night it was his aunt, scarcely older than he was and a dear friend to both of them over the years. He had been strengthened by many people. He was particularly grateful that she was the one with him when the end came.

"Come and have breakfast," she said quietly as they left the hospital, having extended their vigil until they had to make way for the medical staff, who, after their concern and discretion, must get on with their work.

Now they were sitting in a booth of a local family restaurant that stayed open 24 hours a day. Neither of them was hungry, but she sensed that he was not ready to go home yet. She knew he needed to be with someone who didn't expect him to talk. She knew he needed to dip into the land of the living before going home to the land of the dead.

It was suitably a modest breakfast - a muffin and orange juice. He didn't have coffee for fear that it would bring him out of the paralysis he needed to be in. He nibbled slowly at his muffin. He had never known that five raisins could take up such a space in a man's life. Each raisin, as he came upon it, was as big as an apple, and it seemed to take him as long to eat it. Each sip of juice felt that it must be the juice of a thousand oranges. If his emotions had deserted him, his physical senses had not.

He couldn't remember ever being so aware of things going on around him. The smell of coffee and of bacon, the sound of the cash register, the warmth of the waitress's face, smiling through her exhaustion as she worked her way toward the last hour of the graveyard shift. Two truckers in the next booth were discussing last night's hockey game. He didn't follow hockey, and yet he could hear the names and scores, and thought he could probably repeat them in a year's time.

A couple with two sleepy children were making their last stop before taking the Newfoundland ferry. As they talked about what would be going on in Harbour Grace, the images in his head were so clear that he wondered if he had ever lived there.

A waitress joked pleasantly with the truckers and in his mind he heard his wife joking pleasantly with him over breakfast. The truckers joked back and he heard himself joking with his wife in return. It started a flood of images surrounding the breakfasts he had eaten in haste, the breakfasts he had not eaten and the coffee he had drunk on his way out the door. In the midst of the haste and hurry, of the sleepiness and preoccupations with work, there had been intimate moments, just as there were between the waitress and the truckers or the tired couple heading home to Newfoundland. He looked at the sleepy children and thought of his own children home in bed. He looked across the table at his aunt and wondered why she looked like his wife. He had a head full of images now, and was ready to go home to cry.

"Thanks for the breakfast," he said slowly. "I needed that." He walked out with her, knowing that there was enough life in that muffin to take him through the days to come.

"*They'd steal from God* the Father Himself," she thought as she sat listening to the speeches at the twenty-fifth anniversary of the local soup kitchen. She wasn't thinking this of the people who had eaten at the soup kitchen. She was thinking it of the people who were making the speeches.

They were stealing as she listened to them, stealing from the people they were addressing, even as they were being applauded. Like magicians who take your wallet out of your pocket without being seen. The difference is that magicians tell you they're going to take your wallet and they give it back. It's entertainment. No one had been told that this was going to be an evening of entertainment.

What they were stealing, these men at the head table, was not money, at least not here and now. They were stealing something less tangible but just as valuable. They were stealing the credit and the glory for the success of this twenty-five-year-old community project. A project that succeeded because of the dedication and perseverance of community members.

But then, she had to admit to herself when she looked at it more objectively, that there actually was part of the credit these politicians were not stealing. They had earned some of it and they deserved to make their claims. They had used their influence to get the land and building, and they had used their influence to get grants to get the project started. And there had been more grants to keep it going. Some at that table had done nothing more than sign papers that approved the grants, but their signatures were worth a lot, and one had to be humble in front of them.

What she objected to was that there was little mention of all the volunteers who had worked over the years to give this project a human face. The countless hours of sorting out food, preparing it, serving it, cleaning up. The countless hours of repair work, painting, decorating and giving life to the bread. The committee work, the food drives. And, of course, the thousands of people who had contributed and kept the pantry stocked. Their contribution was lumped together in a few short sentences and not one of them was given the opportunity to speak. She wasn't sure whom she was most angry with, the politicians on the stage or the organizers of the event.

And something about the whole evening bothered her even more. It was bad enough that the volunteers were mentioned very little in the history book that was being written at the head table, but it was worse that the people who had eaten here at the centre for twenty-five years were not even mentioned at all. Who were they? They must be important since so many people had spent so much time and energy on them for so many years? If they were worth all this work, there must be something good that could be said about them. If they weren't to speak for themselves, might not someone speak for them? Apparently not.

She thought of the Acadian writer Antoinne Maillet's book *La Sagouine*. The old scrub-woman had a philosophy that would apply here. She claimed it's easier for rich people to get to heaven than it is for poor people. The rich have money to do charity with, and they have all kinds of things to eat so that it is easier for them to do penance. The poor have nothing to give and nothing to cut out. How can they earn their merits? It was something to think about.

And thinking about it made her miss the last speech. The tables were set now and the soup kitchen staff served the meal that they had prepared in honour of the benefactors. It was a simple meal. They had decided to serve the regular fare of the centre. The minister who gave grace pointed out that because of this food there were people in the town and perhaps far beyond who had been given the energy and the hope to do good things for themselves and for others. She felt better after he said that.

But she still wished the regulars could have been there to share in the celebration. She wasn't sure if they would want to, but she decided for the next celebration she would make sure they were asked.

"...He will give you another advocate..."

(John 14:15-21)

She wished she could dump her lawyer and get a new one. She wished her divorce proceedings could simply vanish. She wished her husband would suddenly decide not to contest anything. She wished she had never married. She wished she weren't so tired.

But she was very tired. She wasn't used to fighting. It wore her down to the point where she would have been willing to sign anything just to be alone and not pursued by anyone. It was her unwillingness to fight that had kept her married all these years.

She was very much married and would be so until the final papers were signed. Probably even after the papers were signed, because she still didn't want to be unmarried. She didn't know if she would ever want to be unmarried.

There was no way that her husband would suddenly decide not to contest anything. He was in a fighting mood - as if he had wanted to pick a fight with her all these years, as if his victories had all been too easy. For the first time in all these years he had a decent fight on his hands and she knew he was excited about it. He wasn't going to let go of anything.

The divorce proceedings were not going to vanish. Sometimes she went for whole weeks ignoring homework her lawyer had given her, in the hope that her husband would be kidnapped by aliens, that she would win a lotto, even though she didn't ever buy tickets, or that divorce laws would suddenly change and make these proceedings unnecessary. She always ended up with a lecture from her lawyer for making his work more difficult.

She couldn't dump her lawyer, as little as she liked him. She was already struggling with her payments to him and starting over again would undoubtedly involve more costs. She didn't want to have to go through her story from the beginning all over again. And besides, her lawyer was acting in what he perceived to be her best interests and was competent enough not to allow himself to be swayed by her feelings. After all, if she couldn't trust her own feelings, how could she expect her lawyer to trust her feelings and still do his job.

Her feelings were the problem. Deep down inside herself she felt her lawyer was a heartless man dealing with a cruel system. His job was to come up with the best financial package possible for her. Period. Her husband had to look after himself, and it seemed clear that he was doing just that. Some of the things she had intended for her children would have to be bartered away, but she couldn't have her cake and eat it. Her lawyer was concerned about her cake. That's what she was paying him for, not to sort out her feelings.

Her lawyer sent her to a counsellor because her tears were becoming a nuisance. He didn't tell her, but she reminded him of his own wife who was forever threatening to complicate his life with her tears. He didn't tell her that he gave his wife trips instead of sending her to a counsellor. There was no point in suggesting trips. There was no money for trips — not yet.

The counsellor backed up the lawyer. She would need all of her emotional resources to get through the proceedings. She couldn't afford to waste any resources by being at cross-purposes with her lawyer. Besides, the counsellor reasoned, it was better for her to be hard-nosed now. If she wanted to be generous to her husband and children after the divorce was finalized, there was nothing to prevent her. On the other hand, if she were generous now and changed her mind later, it would be too late.

The counsellor's advice was as heartless as the lawyer's, but she accepted it, partly because the counsellor was a nicer person and partly because they were two against one, both of whom she was paying. How many people could she afford to pay and not take their advice?

She loved her husband but didn't respect him. She loved and respected her children but over-protected them. Her husband was looking for a fight, but was going to feel hurt when he lost. Her children wanted her to stand up for herself, but were going to feel hurt if their father was hurt. They were also going to be disappointed when their property was sold off. She was going to come out of this feeling mean. It was a victory she could not cherish and already she cringed.

She wasn't willing to lose and she was afraid of winning. There was no one who could resolve this for her. In the end, she decided she had been a loser long enough.

"I give you a new commandment..."
John 15:9-17

"*Nobody keeps the* commandments any more," she said accusingly. "Most people don't even know the commandments any more. And the priests aren't much better. They're afraid of preaching on the commandments."

Since she was looking out the kitchen window when this revelation came to her, he assumed that she was not referring to any of the murders that had recently occurred in the area. Perhaps someone was committing adultery on the neighbour's lawn, or at the very least, coveting her new car in the driveway.

It turned out to be neither. It was the kids from up the street taking a short cut through their yard again. He wished the kids wouldn't insist on doing this, but he wished even more that Moses had never written those commandments down in the first place. Everything that went wrong seemed to be directly attributable to the breaking of the commandments, from the recent federal budget to the black knot in the cherry trees. If it was a situation that he could do something about, like the black knot, he was expected to do it right away, before Moses appeared in front of him and smashed the stone tablets at his feet. If it was a situation he could do nothing about, like the federal budget, he was at least expected to feel guilty and perhaps curse the people on welfare and unemployment.

In this case, he could and he couldn't. He had already done something. He had gone out and asked the kids very politely if they would mind taking the long way around. His wife was sick, he told them, and didn't like being disturbed. It

51

wasn't true that she was sick, and by saying this he was breaking another commandment. But he found that you sometimes had to break one commandment in order to keep another. But he had broken the commandment for nothing because it hadn't worked. The kids politely agreed to stop cutting through the yard but they didn't stop. He asked them less politely a second time, without lying, and this time they ran away without saying anything. Then he resorted to screaming at them and threatening to call the police. The kids were still coming through.

Perhaps he should call the police. He didn't think that would work. Perhaps he could call the priest and ask him to preach about the commandments. He wasn't sure what commandment this came under. Surely the priest would know. But he knew he would never ask the priest. And he knew the priest wouldn't do it even if he asked. Even if the priest did, it wouldn't help. The kids were Presbyterians.

He knew what would work, and he knew that was what she wanted him to do. She wanted him to build a tall fence around the back yard. Tall enough that the kids couldn't scale it. He considered it. There was a problem. The people on the back street would completely lose their view of the lake and would be very angry. Although he didn't like to do this to them, he could live with it. The fact was that this was what his wife wanted in the first place. She didn't like the people on the back street, and that was why she wanted the fence. She wouldn't admit it, though, and was using the kids as an excuse. He threatened to build the fence and tell the people on the back street that she wanted them blocked out. She told him to go ahead but he knew he couldn't. That was as far as the situation had gone.

He decided his wife was right about nobody keeping the

commandments and now was as good a time as any to do something about it. He would start with honesty, which he figured probably came under the one about false witness. He would go and have a talk with the parents of the kids and see if they could resolve the issue peacefully.

It wouldn't resolve the question about the fence. He figured that came under the one about loving your neighbour as yourself, but he didn't feel ready to tackle that one. He'd have to start with his wife first, and he doubted that they would ever get around to the fence.

"I am going away, and shall return..."

John 14:23-29

"*How far do I have to go* to get away from him?" he asked himself as he sat at the kitchen table of his apartment in the city of Vancouver. From the kitchen window he looked out across the tops of houses at the Pacific Ocean. To get farther away he would have to cross that ocean. He had never been very good at geography, but he figured that if he crossed the ocean it would take him to China or some place on the other side of the world, and then he might be getting closer to his home in Cape Breton, coming at it from the other side. He wasn't going to bother going to the public library to look it up on the globe, because he wasn't going to go to China anyway. He'd be lucky if he could save up enough money to get to Calgary for his holidays, to spend some time with the boys from back home.

It just wasn't working out. He'd been here for a year now, and he wasn't making any headway. He had not found a steady job, and the holiday that he was taking in Calgary was not really a holiday. He was going to be out of work and he was going to Calgary to see if the boys there might be able to find him something. He was going to sublet his apartment in Vancouver because he didn't want to give it up. Even if it wasn't much of an apartment, it had a view of the ocean. And even though he wanted to get away from his father, he didn't want to get away from the ocean. He couldn't imagine Calgary ever being a pemanent home for him.

He thought of his father now, and wondered what kind of power his father had over him. "If you'd gone to school, if you'd

54

listened to me, if your mother hadn't spoiled you." If, if, if . . .
"If you'd gotten off my back," he thought, "I might be back in
Cape Breton, I might be a school teacher like yourself, and I
might even have listened to you. I tried. And it's not true that
my mother spoiled me. She listened to me. If you had listened
to her, perhaps, or if she had hit you on the head with a frying
pan, if, if, if..."

It wasn't working. The more he argued with his father in
his head, the bigger his father got and the smaller he felt. If he
kept this up he'd soon feel no bigger than a rabbit. There was
nothing here he would be proud to show his father - a job he
didn't like that would soon be over, a grungy apartment, and no
social life. His father would laugh at him.

He had to get his mind off the "ifs". The "ifs" were killing
him, bringing him down. From being the size of a rabbit, he'd
get down to the size of a frog, then a grasshopper, then . . . He
had to connect with something real in his life. He looked out the
window at the ocean. That was real.

The ocean was real, and his books were real. Not that he
had many books, but the few that he had were wonderful. They
opened up a whole new world. Not like the stupid books his
father read, when he read at all. Not like the stupid books his
father hadn't read himself but tried to get him to read. No, these
were good books. And if he couldn't afford to buy many, there
was the public library and the bookstores. He loved the bookstores. There were so many of them and they were so exciting.
All the interesting ideas that came in from China and India and
Tibet and everywhere. If he didn't know where China was on
the map, he certainly knew a lot about the people who lived
there. And the native peoples of British Columbia. He wondered
why he had never learned much about the native people in Cape
Breton.

It was strange that the more he looked at the ocean, the more he thought of his books, and how good he felt about them. It occurred to him that in his own way he was becoming educated, and it was a process that pleased him. Someday maybe he would go to university, but he wasn't ready yet, and it wasn't important to him now.

He decided he didn't need to go any farther to get away from his father. In fact, he didn't need to get away from his father at all. What he needed was to get closer to himself. And he could do that with his books. And someday when he had read enough, he would return to Cape Breton. The ocean was there and perhaps he would find more good books there too, now that he knew what to look for.

He might even be able to hold his own with his father.

It was festival time again and he didn't know whether to laugh or cry.

He loved the festival. Winter was so long and early spring was so dreary that it seemed as if his blood had curdled. The only time he heard a fiddle was at funerals, the only time he smelled real flowers was at funerals, and the only time he talked to people outside his own family was at work. He didn't play darts or cards, and he didn't go to church, except for funerals. He wondered if he didn't go to church because he didn't get to talk to people there anyway, at least not in the winter time, when everyone scrambled quickly to get into their cars. Whatever the reason, visiting neighbours, home and school, and square dances were no longer part of his life.

But when the wild pear burst into bloom and people started mowing their lawns, he got festival fever. It was a time for celebration. Music, eating and drinking, but mostly people. People who came from all over the place to celebrate with them. People who camped on the beach, people who barbecued at their cottages or in the picnic parks, people who came to play ball, to swim and to sail, people who stopped to take pictures, people who had never been to a milling frolic or a ceilidh . . . this went on all summer, of course, but not as intensely as it did during the festival. He even went to church during the festival, and enjoyed it too, probably because people talked to one another before and after Mass. And the Mass itself seemed exciting.

He enjoyed the preparation too. After all, the festival required a lot of preparation, a lot of work for months beforehand. But he liked doing his share, and he realized that it was really the only opportunity he had to spend time with other people in the community, to get to know them or keep in touch with the ones he had grown up with. There were a lot of laughs, a lot of stories, a lot of warmth and sharing. He delighted in it and ate it up, aware of how hungry he had been for it all winter, how lean his life was without neighbours in it.

It was also a problem. If the neighbours saved up their appreciation of one another throughout the winter, they also saved up their little resentments. Everything that they had disapproved of during the winter but hadn't had a chance to say came out one way or another. Sometimes the stories weren't as funny as they were hurtful. Sometimes the neighbours working together disagreed bitterly on something insignificant. There had to be something else behind it, but nobody was saying. And when a piece was taken out of you, it was usually in public, where it was difficult to defend yourself.

At times like this he lost sight of the wild pear blossoms and couldn't hear the melody of the fiddles. At times like this the little village felt like a huge city, full of violence and hatred and hurts. At times like this he wanted to chuck it all and go fishing, and settle for fiddle music on his cassette player.

But the people were in his blood, as much as the fiddles and the wild pear, and he knew that, come festival time, he could sit in church with them again and feel at home.

"The family has to be fed," was

the answer he gave to those who questioned him about his going away year after year to work on the lake boats.

He wasn't quite satisfied with his answer, and that was why he got a bit uncomfortable when anyone asked. His answer was true, but it was only part of a greater truth.

He felt somehow that his answer was a grudging admission that he wasn't as good a husband and parent as he ought to be, that he wasn't as good a parent as the men who had jobs at home, and that his main role in the family was to provide an income, "to put bread on the table."

That just wasn't true, and he felt disappointed in himself for selling himself short. The truth was that he was a very good husband and parent, and he was never really absent from his family. For one thing they never allowed him to leave without them. They always loaded him down with pictures, souvenirs, and memorabilia of all sorts, from sports trophies to favourite seashells and pressed flowers. They followed him with mail that awaited him whenever he came into port, and they in turn awaited his phone calls.

They were in his thoughts every day while he was away. He thought of what they were doing and his thoughts were fuelled by the letters they wrote. He shared their eagerness and their excitement about everyday events and marvelled at how he was able to imagine everything that was going on without actually being there. He worried when they sounded troubled and continued to carry their troubles with him long after they had actually disappeared. He would ask immediately about these troubles when he got to a phone. The children would shrug them off, and his wife would give him an account of what had happened. It was history for them now, but they all felt pleased and proud that their troubles had been shared. From his side, he saw everything through their eyes. Having lived on the water most of his life, he saw deeply into the depths — the depths of the water and the depths of the lives he shared. In that way, they were with him.

There was another part of him that didn't belong to his family, and perhaps that was the part that gave him a twinge of guilt until he realized how important it was to him, and how much he liked it. He had grown up in a family of sea-going men, and this tradition went back more generations than he could trace. There was much about the water that he could share, but he couldn't share living on the water. It could be shared only with others who lived on the water too. These people formed a community of their own. There was an unspoken bond among them, and between them and the water. The community lived outside of the world of business, politics, and organization. It was affected by business, politics and organizations, dependent on business, politics and organizations and aware of its dependence on them. Still it had a life of its own.

This way of life was changing, the very water itself was changing. But so far, there was still a part of it that was only sailors, boats, and water. A person could get lost and found in this world, a person could get born and reborn in this a million times over, as surely as if he were being immersed into a baptismal font. The water was a major sacrament in his life. The sailors shared this sacrament, conferred it upon one another.

He was always home for the winter, usually in time for Christmas. His family had him all to themselves then. But they only had him because he came home a happy man, brimming with life. Immersed in water, he left the water just before it froze. It continued to run, with his blood, throughout his veins for the whole winter. His family was fed in many ways, winter and summer, and so was he.

But it was only June now and a long way to Christmas. He wondered what they were doing at home. Next Sunday was Father's Day. Perhaps his daughter, at this very moment, was drawing him a Father's Day card. Now might be a good time to work on the wooden mermaid that he was carving for her. It was the most complicated piece he had ever done and a good time to get at it, while he felt himself so strongly attached to both land and water.

"He will not be speaking as from Himself..."

(John 16:12-15)

$She\ looked\ at\ the$ coal miner's lamp that she kept on a shelf in the corner of the living room. She was not sure why she kept it there, for she was not a particularly sentimental woman. Her husband had been dead for twenty years now, and although he was still real to her, he was not real to her as a miner. When she read the daily accounts of the Westray Mine disaster in the newspaper, and when she saw the faces of the miners' widows, she grieved for them, and not for her husband. Her husband had not died in a mining accident nor of a mine-related disease. He had died of heart failure while on vacation. It would have happened whether he worked as a shoe maker or a stock broker. No, when she thought of her husband, it was of him fixing a bicycle, strumming the guitar, or playing tarabish. She did not associate him with disaster of any kind, or with the more serious aspects of life. He had died before being exposed to the darker side of life.

And so the lamp wasn't really his. At times she wasn't sure whether it was really hers because she wasn't a miner's wife anymore. Her husband was dead, and sometimes she didn't even feel that she was a miner's widow. She felt for the miners' widows, but she couldn't really say that she was one of them.

And yet the miner's lamp had a very important place in her home and in her life. If she wasn't sure why she kept it, she was very sure that she could never dispose of it. It had a life of its own. It was like a religious object, a statue, or more like a Russian icon. She had seen a program on television about

Russian icons, these curious religious figures, flat and severe looking, but painted in such a way that a light seemed to come out of them, a light that seemed much brighter for coming out of the severity. The miner's lamp was like that, dull and severe when it was new, now having the added dullness of age. It was never lit anymore, so it was just dull. Yet there was a glow that seemed to come from it which she not only saw but felt.

It occurred to her as she sat looking at the lamp that it made her feel, not so much like a miner's wife or widow, but like a miner. She put on the lamp to go down into the depths of her inner self, into her own darkness. She knew the geography of the Cape Breton coal mines, she knew the language, she had heard the stories. She had always been fascinated by the fact that the mines ran out miles underneath the ocean, and she imagined what it must be like to be in the depths of the earth with the sea raging over your head, unheard by you.

And so it was that she sometimes left the turbulence of the sea, the storms of life, the shipping activity, and the cod wars, donned her miner's lamp, and went underground into herself. Not as an escape, mind you, for there were dangers down below as surely as there were dangers above. The Westray mine disaster had reminded her of that only too clearly. But if the dangers were as great underground, there was also a greater sense of knowing what they were, of understanding them, of knowing what you were up against and of coming to terms with it. Greater clarity. It was strange, when she thought of it, that things should be clearer underground, in the dark, than they were in the bright light of day.

That was what she felt about herself. Life wasn't easier when she looked deep into herself, but she felt that it was clearer.

She felt she understood the dangers better and she felt stronger, both when she was inside and when she came up to the surface. She remembered reading a line from the Psalms which said, "A lamp to my feet is Your word, a light to my path," and wondered if the psalm writer had been a coal miner. She didn't know whether they had coal mines in Israel. It wasn't important. She knew the lamp in the corner of the living room was a light for her feet and her path, and for that she thanked all miners everywhere.

$\mathcal{A}$ *dam had broken* inside of him. He felt a torrent of life rushing through him, sweeping debris aside. The torrent was joined by a thousand rivulets from forgotten corners of his body and soul like the ancient Nile River in spring, overflowing its banks and flooding a delta that had lain dry during a long winter. The torrent drew strength from the direction of his feet from where he seemed to make contact with the underground rivers of the earth. From there it moved upward, sweeping through to his hands and mouth, compelling him to embrace the world.

He had not expected this. He was a singer who had learned to sing quietly and only inside himself. His songs were mainly about his childhood, about awe and admiration, about laughter and delight. They were about a time of innocence and purity and about a time of love. But this time had been followed by another time, a time of cloud and darkness, a time of pain and doubt. He couldn't remember the pain anymore or what it was about, but he lived in its shadow, and like the groundhog, he always returned to the darkness of his cave after a quick peek at the sun.

He was a fisherman and most of his life he lived in quiet anonymity with other fishermen and the ocean. The other fishermen left him alone because he was a quiet type. The ocean nursed his songs, the songs which had receded into his depths beyond the reach of pain and cloud. The ocean provided melody for his songs, sometimes gentle, sometimes fierce, always vibrant. There were many songs, as many as the colours and sounds of the ocean.

When he came to shore he lived in a boarding house where he got drunk for two days until it was time to go back to the sea. He lived with an elderly couple who could offer only sympathy since they had no idea how to help him. They were no strangers to drinking, having raised two rebellious sons themselves. At least he was a quiet drunk, which was more than could be said of their own sons. When he sobered up and returned to the water, he felt ashamed of his behaviour. He wondered how the couple ever put up with him. He promised himself it would never happen again. But by the time his boat was safely into the harbour, his resolve had disappeared like the early morning fog.

Sometimes when he was drunk he sang for the couple. His voice wasn't at its best then, and the feelings didn't always match the lyrics, but still the melody was always pleasant and the words true. The couple listened to him patiently, and gradually the woman learned some of the songs herself and sang them as she worked quietly in her kitchen.

Sometimes when he arrived home from the boat, still sober, he found her singing one of his songs. In his embarrassment he would generally find an excuse to leave the house, but secretly he was pleased to hear his songs being sung by someone else. Until he met this elderly couple, he had always been dismissed as a drunk when he sang his songs. He noticed, too, that the woman's husband became more attentive to his wife when she was singing.

Time passed and the woman began to ask him for verses or words that she was missing. At first he resisted because she had developed the habit of asking before he started drinking. It was difficult enough to hear his own songs being sung by someone else. It was much more difficult to hear himself singing them without the protection of a few drinks. And yet his songs were all he had, and he found it painful to hear them sung wrong.

He gave her the words and eventually he sang them for her without a drink. He began singing more and drinking less.

The woman had accepted his drunken singing. Now the torrent which was his singing, and his life, was breaking through. It was not long after that he left the elderly couple. The little room and the little house could no longer contain him. But he visited often, and in between his visits the woman sang his songs while her husband hummed the tune.

The concert was into its fourth hour now and there was no end in sight. The earth itself seemed to be breathing out the music. The concert field was like a huge vibrating tuning fork which the fiddlers had only to listen to and allow their wrists and fingers to follow.

If the actual concert had been going for four hours, the concert field had been warming up long before the concert began. Warming up literally, for the day had moved from a cool fresh morning to a teasingly warm noon to a roasting mid-afternoon when the concert began. The field had warmed up in other ways too, with anticipation and activity. People had begun to arrive even before noon, with motor homes and trunks spilling out coolers, folding chairs, cassette recorders and picnic baskets. These were the organized ones, searching out the prime real estate with the instinct of artic wolves. They looked for level ground, for a good view, for best sound or for privacy. They set up awnings, they laid out checkered tablecloths and covered them with salads, dips and desserts. They brought out cards and they played tarabish, scat or forty-fives, depending on where they were from. They refreshed themselves with Kool-Aid, coolers and mysterious drinks from bottles stored in brown paper bags. Most importantly, they activated their music molecules by playing their favourite fiddlers on their cassette recorders. All the while they socialized with friends and strangers alike.

Unknowingly these early arrivals made a significant contribution to the direction the concert would take. When the people began to arrive in large numbers, they did not enter a wasteland. There was already a settlement here. The field was already lived in. It was already home, and the anxieties and frustrations they had brought with them from home, the stress of trying to be on time, was quickly absorbed by the happy community that greeted them as if it had been awaiting their arrival.

It was this highly receptive community that greeted the musicians when they arrived on the scene. Theirs was the task of bringing focus to the energy that bubbled over the field. A genius had organized the program to begin with a medley of tunes played on the bagpipes. The pipes somehow combine the seductiveness of the snake charmer with the command of the old time school teacher. After ten minutes of piping, from slow air to reel, the crowd was charmed, enthused and instructed like a grade two pupil made ready for a fairy tale.

The fairy tale had already been unfolding for hours now during which the crowd had been taken through many adventures, some indulging in adventures of their own. But the music was strong and the focus remained. At this point the field was like a huge tuning fork. This was total music.

A cloud had moved over the fiery sun in late afternoon and now turned into a cloudburst. People ran for non-existent shelter. For the tired and the old of all ages, it was an excuse to go. But they left happy even as they left wet. They had had as much as they wanted. A good number of people wore sun hats or carried parasols which they could count on for protection if the rain did not last too long. These sat smiling and smug. Still others saw an opportunity to splash about. Rain and music are both liberating forces. Joined together they can allow people to really cut loose. A man and his small children jumped up and began a spirited dance in a large puddle that had formed on a now deserted part of the field. In bare feet, with rain streaming from their faces, they looked like a study of successful rain dancers in National Geographic.

It was to them and to a soggy remnant sitting on the benches that the musicians played for another hour. These last devotees wanted more and they got as much as they wanted. Eventually the musicians stopped playing and everyone went home, leaving a rain- and music-drenched field, fertilized more richly than with nitrogen, to lie fallow for another year.

"one pearl of great value..."
(Matthew 13:44-52)

From the age of eight he had the profound conviction that he had been called to be a monk.

That was in the fifties, when Don Messer, "Father Knows Best," and "Leave It to Beaver" were all supportive of young boys' altruistic visions. His parents used to take him and the other children for Sunday afternoon drives that had the local monastery as a destination.

He loved the monastery. Such a magnificent farm — the trees, meadows, gardens, flowers, animals. There was always more than the senses could take in, and the anticipation kept him in a state of high excitement. The children were permitted to visit the barns and to wander down by the brook while the parents visited the vegetable and flower gardens. Then a walk through a wooded path tracing the stations of the cross. At the end was the sharing of treats from a family picnic basket as a calming exercise before everyone went to the monastery chapel for afternoon benediction. Here the monks suddenly materialized from barns, kitchens, libraries and all the other secret places in the bowels of the monastery. Like birds to a feeder they came, in their flowing robes and cowls, with much bowing and genuflecting, called as if by instinct to the sound of the bell.

He couldn't remember exactly what happened at benediction, but he could remember billows of pleasant-smelling smoke, rich vestments, sonorous organ music, and Latin incantations. At some point he went to sleep and dreamt of himself swathed in robes and swinging pots of smoke, followed about the farmyard by little pigs and ducklings. His mother would wake him and they would leave. He would be well on his way home before the ducklings left him and the dream ended.

But that was in the fifties, and by the time he was old enough to become a monk, the calendar had moved on to the late sixties and the monastery of his youth no longer existed. The buildings of the monastery were still there, but the monks were old and no longer worked the farm. They mechanized it at first. But even that was too much work, and they leased their land to a local farmer. They hardly ever wore their flowing robes, and there was no one to play the organ anymore. There were only a few old birds at the feeder, and they came without even the call of bells.

There had been a social revolution too, so that the notions of obedience and celibacy had taken a bad beating. He thought he might deal with celibacy, but there didn't seem to be anyone around worth obeying. And so he married.

His marriage lasted only long enough to produce a daughter. Somehow he had forgotten to tell his wife that the one vow he kept without making it was poverty. She tired very quickly of his lack of interest in getting ahead. He had no one to blame but himself, and he blessed her and apologized to her as she went on her way.

Now it was the nineties and he had come close to full circle. For three years he had been living in what was really a monastery. All that was missing were the monks. He occupied his monastery alone. He had sold what few assets he had and bought an old farm, to which he added a horse, a cow, a few sheep, hens, ducks and a dog. He had a garden and a woodlot, from which he cut his own firewood, and some pulpwood to provide a small income for himself.

His own monastery. He had all the vital signs of life around him that had captured his soul more than thirty years before. He had the animals, giving of their produce and giving birth. He sold the produce and he sold some of the animals but not before all of it had gone through his own hands. He tended the gardens, and he filled his freezers. He worked with the rhythms of nature.

He did not build the Stations of the Cross in the woods, but he found himself thinking of them often enough as he walked up the road to his woodlot. Nature could be more demanding than any father superior and at least as unreasonable. And although he worked for no earthly boss, he had to answer regularly to a number of government agencies that could be as cold as Pilate and as devious as Judas. At least Pilate and Judas had had faces for Jesus to confront and challenge. Often he found himself having to confront and challenge computers — machines with not even the heart of a Pilate or a Judas. No, he didn't need visible stations. He found it difficult to pray alone, and he found it difficult to eat alone. He longed for human company. He even wondered if he should join the old monks. He had found a pearl of great value, but it was also a pearl of great price.

"You have plenty of good things laid by..."

(Luke 12:13-21)

His money was stuck to him like burdocks, and he couldn't get rid of it. He cursed it silently.

It didn't make sense. In a world where there was so much good waiting to be done, where there were so many needy people, it was ridiculous that he not be able to spend his few miserable dollars. It was more than a few actually, ninety-four thousand to be exact. At least that's what it had been on his last bank statement. By now it would be a few dollars more. He didn't have to feed it. It grew quietly from day to day. It had a life of its own and all he could do with it was continue to watch it grow. What stopped him from spending his money was the ghost of his dead wife.

She had been dead a year now but she had not left his side for even a day. Not for a night either, for that matter, as he dreamed of her every night. Tall, slender with white hair freshly permed, she stood there silently. He couldn't make out her features clearly, by day or night, and that weighed heavily upon him, like a curse. To think that he had been married to this woman for forty-four years and was not able to picture her face troubled him deeply. He would resort to the picture albums where he would search out her many faces - happy, sad, tired, excited, laughing. There he could see her clearly and feel confident that her face would never disappear from his memory. But disappear it did, each time he closed the picture albums. Only her form would remain, the tall slender body and the immaculately white hair. He tried to make her speak, but she had no voice. No voice and no face.

He had known something was wrong between them immediately after she died. He recognized it in the very act of selecting her coffin. Without a moment's hesitation he had picked the most exquisite piece in the funeral parlour show room. Cool, rich mahogany, long and slender to match her long and slender body. And in the moment of picking it, he had seen that same coffin as a mahogany diningroom set with her sitting elegantly at the head of the table. He knew then that he had sinned. The brass handles on the coffin became brass lamps, the satin lining became billowing satin drapes, and the sin turned into pain.

Months later, when the time came to select a headstone for her grave, he thought he would do it differently and buy something attractive and simple rather than act out of what he felt must be guilt. But in the end he was unable to resist buying the tall shapely marble stone with the curlicues. There was almost enough marble in it to build a banister.

It became clear to him that the money he had saved on her in life, he found himself compelled to spend on her in death.

But that was it. He had run out of ways to spend money on her. He thought of setting up a scholarship fund in her name. He thought of giving a generous donation to the church, but neither seemed right. As he had not been generous to the world around him when she was living, he doubted she would be impressed with such a gesture now. He thought of giving his money to his children instead of leaving it to them when he died, but he couldn't bring himself to do that. One of the children was a copy of himself and already had fat bank accounts of his own. The other two were spendthrifts and would squander it foolishly in front of his eyes.

Sometimes he became angry with his wife. It hadn't been fair of her to just up and die on him. He had always assumed they would enjoy a comfortable old age together, she would outlive him, and he would leave her well provided for. She could even have had her mahogany dining set after he died. He could have smiled down from heaven and approved of his stately widow.

Now he had nothing to approve of, just a bunch of money that he couldn't spend–money that kept growing in defiance of him–and a faceless ghost that haunted his days and nights. He had only one hope left. He began to pray to her that she would show her face and speak to him.

The storm had damaged his boat. Not extensively, not enough to stop him from going out—it could be repaired later, when the fishing season was over. More importantly, it was work that he could do himself. It could have been much worse—it had in fact been much worse for several others. Two of them were tied up for the rest of the season.

The wharf had been damaged, because the breakwater protecting it was in need of repairs and upgrading, and it was a difficult time to pry money loose for upgrading when there might not be any fishing at all in a few years. At least not from this particular harbour. It had always been a poor harbour, and it was only through a great deal of fighting that the fishermen had ever gotten it developed at all. There had been fishing here as long as anyone could remember; but in his father's and his grandfather's times, the men had gone out only under ideal conditions. There were lots of fish then, and you could make a living even if you didn't get out all the time. But times had changed and the support systems had disappeared. A man needed to fish all the time or get out. The breakwater had made that possible, although it also meant taking higher risks. And bigger boats meant bigger repairs. Everything had gotten bigger, except the fish catches.

As he looked at the boat, he knew that he could repair it. But as he arrived at this conclusion, he experienced something that he had never experienced before. A wave of doubt came over him—doubt in the boat and doubt in himself. Something had happened during this long debate over the fish stocks and the viability of the fishing industry. Something had disappeared that was not going to come back, even if somehow the fish stocks were miraculously returned to their previous level. He was never going to feel the same way he had felt about himself as a fisherman. The way his father and grandfather had felt about themselves as fishermen. And their fathers before them.

He was being seen as a predator, in the same way grey seals, factory ships and manufacturers of industrial waste were seen as predators. The reports weren't all in yet but responsibility for the fish decline was already being apportioned, and no one involved was escaping.

It had shocked him to be compared with a grey seal. The factory ship and the pollutants were probably more destructive, so much more so that he could feel morally superior to them. But a grey seal was personal—you could put a face on it. His grandfather must be turning in his grave. The world was going to hell in a basket when a grey seal could look you in the eye as an equal, his grandfather would say.

It was a good thing his grandfather wasn't around. Some people might agree that a grey seal was indeed as important as a fisherman. Thinking about it now, he could see a certain logic to it, but it certainly blew a hole in the image his family had had of itself for hundreds of years. Fishing had been an honourable way of life, sacred, a vocation. Right, a vocation. He remembered, from his childhood days, the priest talking in his Sunday sermon about vocations. The priest had given examples of vocations—a priest, a doctor, a fisherman. Only his grandfather had reversed the order—a fisherman, a doctor, a priest. You could get along without the priest, and the doctor wasn't much good to you if you didn't have anything to eat. Fisherman first, definitely. That's the way it had always been.

He wondered how the priest must be feeling now and whether the priest would be willing to give his pulpit over to the grey seal. The thought seemed funny to him, and he laughed out loud. And then he imagined the seal's face, and he thought the seal was laughing too.

As he laughed with the seal, he realized that the seal was not the enemy. It was not the seal that was battering him about. He and the seal were competitors who had always fought one another with respect. He, the seal, the fish—they were all being battered by a system, a faceless system that had reduced them all to an economic game. And once again he had come close to drowning, to accepting the number assigned to him by the system.

Well, he wasn't drowned yet, and didn't plan to be. He'd repair his boat, he'd fish as long as he could, and then he'd see. But as long as he lived he'd never see the day that he couldn't look a seal, a codfish, or another man in the eye.

She didn't like her dentist. He would not have been her dentist except for the fact that he was the only dentist in town, and it was too far for her to travel elsewhere. Besides, he was a skilled surgeon and she kept reminding herself that she went to him to have her teeth fixed and not for a relationship.

Today was not a good day. She had gone for a job interview as secretary of the newly formed Community Council Against Violence. The interview had not gone well. She had been at a disadvantage from the beginning. The chairman of the interviewing committee had met her at the door and shaken hands with her while looking her over as if she might be a prospective model for two piece bathing suits. His study had been very brief, and he had ushered her quickly inside the room without as much as scanning her face, let alone looking her in the eyes. She was very conscious of her weight and had an immediate sinking feeling. She felt better when she met the other two members of the committee, a man and a woman, both pleasant, warm and relaxed.

But whatever advantage she thought she had was quickly lost with the beginning of the interview. She had hoped to impress them with her record of work with community organizations and particularly her work as secretary of the Home and School Association. The questioning had taken another direction, focusing on her professional experience in the formal work force. She had very little. She had spent all her adult life raising her children. She could not bring the committee around to look at her strengths. And she had felt the interview going down the drain. She had left discouraged. She would be notified about the job, but she felt she already knew the answer.

Now her dentist was working on her teeth and at the same time sending little sermons directly into her mouth and down her throat. She was finding the sermons hard to swallow. They were getting mixed in with her saliva, and she was gagging on both.

The sermons weren't actually delivered as sermons but in the form of a dialogue, for the dentist kept asking her questions. It was difficult, however, with her mouth filled with equipment and the dentist's both hands, to give much of a response. The dentist would wait a few seconds and then, interpreting her silence as assent, would go forward with the next stage of his argument. The topic today was education, for he too was aware of violence, and he saw the education system as being at fault. He talked about the values he had learned when he had gone to school and to university, and of how much he owed his teachers. Being herself a product of the old system, she tried to remember if she had ever seen him at a Home and School meeting, which had been so much part of the system he was talking about. She had not, and in fact, she had not seen or heard from him in any of the many community organizations she had been involved with.

She wanted to scream, but now he was drilling, and she had visions of him slicing off her tongue if she as much as made a move. The drill reverberated down into her tooth, her jaw, her throat, her chest and into her heart.

She opened her eyes, which she had kept closed in order to ward off Phil Donahue and all his guests from joining the dentist and the equipment in her mouth. There was a television hanging from the ceiling directly above her face. What she saw instead was the bright light that the dentist had placed between her face and the television set to enable him to follow more clearly the movement of his drill into her heart. She followed the light from its source and allowed it to enter her and eventually to envelop her heart.

The sound of the drill, and the sermons, began to fade into the distance. As her heart lit up, it began to emit light itself, light that slowly radiated in every direction, filling first her chest cavity and then moving outward to illuminate her whole body. She saw the heart of a caring person, a heart that could protect and heal victims of violence. She saw the heart of a committed person, a heart that had already guided her through years of service. There was no drill, dentist or committee that could gag this heart.

She breathed deeply and relaxed, looking forward to going home to tell her children that she was ready to go to work.

Sometimes she regretted that she was no longer baking her own bread. She knew it didn't make sense any more. She couldn't very well give up her job to stay home and bake bread. She needed to work because of the money, and she needed to do something that gave her more satisfaction than staying home and doing chores. Baking bread after work was not possible because there were so many other things to be done. Besides, she could afford to buy bread that was actually better than the bread she used to make.

She was just being romantic about something that, at the time she was doing it, had been just another chore. And yet, romance or not, there had been something satisfying about it. She thought about it—hands in the dough, hands in the dough.

"Was it the power my hands had when they were in the dough?" The images started to come.

"I could never caress my children but I swear they felt caressed when I listened to their stories and caressed the dough. My hands would pause in the dough, work it slowly as the children hesitated, their eyes eagerly watching the dough for signs of encouragement. Sometimes the dough would stop with them and wait until it was safe to go on. When they started again, the dough would start with them, working up courage. The story would become stronger and magically finish at the same time I gave a firm pat to a finished loaf. There. All done now. Watch it rise.

My hands in the dough won many an argument too. The things they encouraged me to say, the things I didn't have to say to get my point across, as my hands pounded the dough, slapped it in disapproval. People knew what I was talking about.

There were tears I never could have shed without the dough. My sister could always tell. It was when I handled the dough as gently as if it were a newborn baby. What I was comforting was my own troubled soul, which could not bear any roughness or carelessness at that moment. My sister would watch the dough and carefully bring me around to talking about my problem."

And so each loaf had been a gift. A gift of her caresses, a gift of her anger, a gift of her tears. All worked through with her hands. This was what she regretted—not having a way to get herself involved as easily as she had with her hands in the dough.

Yet when she thought about it she realized that, through the years, she had learned to caress her children, she had learned to express her anger in a positive way that no longer hurt her friends. She had learned to comfort herself and allow herself to be comforted.

The gift was herself and she was able now to give it without the bread. She gave it so many times, every day, not only in what she did for others but in who she was, in tears and in laughter.

Still, she wasn't sure she would ever have done it without the bread. She figured it wasn't necessary to make bread all your life, but maybe everyone should have to learn how to do it— make bread for a given number of years. Maybe it should be taught to all young girls and boys along with reading and basketball.

For even if she didn't make it any more, she still had a tremendous respect for a fine loaf of bread and it gave her more pleasure than most things she could imagine.

"...and they watched him closely..."
(Luke 14:1,7-14

From their corner of the room they had an almost perfect view. The door was directly across from them and a short distance away. They could see people arrive and they could see people leave. They could see who arrived with whom and who didn't arrive. They could see the expressions on people's faces as they arrived and they could see the expression on people's faces as they left. The bar and kitchen were also across from them and next to the door. They could watch people gather around the bar, and best of all, they could see directly into the kitchen.

The kitchen was a good indicator of how the evening was going. The workers in the kitchen commented to one another on the activities around the hall and on guests as they left the kitchen counter with their food. The kitchen workers were free to do this since they weren't part of the evening's activity, and the guests were too busy doing their own thing to pay much attention to them.

The head table at the other end of the hall was raised on a dias so that the head table guests were visible from all parts of the hall. The head table guests themselves didn't enjoy such a view. They could look down on the main body of the hall, but they couldn't see into the kitchen, and they couldn't see the entrance to the hall because it was hidden by the kitchen and bar.

Finally, the corner facing the door had a table that seated only two people, so that its occupants could both sit with their backs to the wall. It was a most suitable spot for a couple of voyeurs.

86

They had not, of course, been assigned to this table in order to be voyeurs. They had been assigned to this table because it was the greatest possible distance from the head table and the least likely spot to become a focus of attention. She was a sister of the man being honoured at the head table. Her brother and his wife didn't like her and yet had felt compelled to invite her and her husband for the sake of appearance. They had been relegated to the corner. It had all been carefully planned — to keep up appearances.

The man being honoured was retiring. He was accompanied at the head table by his wife and business colleagues. The surrounding tables were for children and grandchildren, followed by a line of community organization representatives heading discreetly toward the corner. The other side of the hall was occupied by all those who did not fit into any particular category. To those who were not aware of the family dynamics, it looked innocent enough and quite agreeable. Everyone, after all, cannot sit at or around the head table. Someone has to sit at the opposite end and someone has to sit in corners. In a true community a seating arrangement is not an issue. This was not a true community, and it had been done in a spirit of meanness.

The mean-spirited gesture did not work, however, because the sister and her husband did not co-operate. They were not used to being victims. It didn't suit them. They always managed to turn situations to their own advantage. In this case, they immediately saw how easy it was to be voyeurs, and they quickly settled into the role. They enjoyed themselves watching everything that was going on in different areas of the hall. They shared insights with one another, they gossiped and they laughed. Unnoticed by the head table at first, they devoted themselves to having a quiet good time.

The good time lasted the whole evening, but it became less quiet. Their enjoyment spread, and brought back more enjoyment to meet it. As the head table speeches finished and the evening became more informal, people began to drop by the corner table to chat. Eventually two couples pulled their tables over to the corner so that they could all sit together. By then they were being watched closely from the head table, but it was too late. The speeches over, the head table guests had little in common to animate the conversations. People dropped by the head table, but only to pay their respects. They did not know the head table guests well and besides, the honoree's wife was now quite distracted with watching the activities in the far corner.

In the end, the corner table looked too much like the head table, and the couple who had first occupied it alone got up and started mixing discreetly among other guests throughout the hall.

He had been waiting for the bomb to drop. He didn't know where, he didn't know when. All he knew was that it would happen. The signs were there. Like a Baked Alaska in reverse. The coolness was on the outside. The frost was in the smile and in the movements. But it barely served to cover the fire that burned fiercely underneath. Something was wrong with his sister, and the world was going to find out about it one of these days.

He wished it weren't this way. He liked his sister. He wished he could walk up to her and ask her what was eating her up. But it wasn't easy. They hadn't been brought up to be open. There was a family protocol that one followed, a politic. And it didn't allow for anger. Brothers and sisters were expected to be nice to one another, not angry. They failed, of course, to live up to this expectation. They did get angry with one another, but they rarely showed it. And when they did show it, it was in outbursts, like electric storms. You could see the clouds gathering on the horizon, darkening. You could feel the air pressure lowering. The storms would come. Everyone would hide under the table until it was over and come out again when the air cleared. By that time, everyone was relieved to get back to normal, so relieved that they didn't care to discuss the issue that had caused the storm in the first place. Everyone lived happily ever after, or at least until the next storm. It was the typical perfect family.

She caught him totally by surprise this time. She came to his house and told him that she wanted to speak to him. He got frightened. This was out of character for her. No one in his family had ever planned the setting for a storm or a bombing before. Her coming would make it more difficult to get away. How could he hide under the table if she was going to be sitting there looking at him. Unplanned storms make it easier to run for cover. The storm was too caught up with itself to notice what others were doing. Besides, she was already heading for the living room and the only table there was a coffee table. He could never hide under that table. He wished he were Alice in Wonderland and could make himself smaller.

He offered a cup of tea but she declined. No social niceties, no props. He made a quick move towards the rocking chair, but she blocked it off and claimed it for herself. He wasn't going to be allowed to comfort himself by rocking. She wasn't going to rock either. She sat in the chair upright. The chair moved slightly either way on its rockers and came to a complete standstill.

She came directly to the point. He had been visiting her house more often than usual lately. And he had managed to have his visits coincide with the visits of her best girlfriend. The girlfriend was married. And on several occasions he had even managed to organize a little party to which both the girlfriend and her husband were invited. She did not know whether the girlfriend was aware of her brother's movements yet. But her girlfriend was going to know because she was going to tell her. She was here first to serve notice of what she was going to do.

He wondered why she wasn't screaming. He wished she would. This storm was all lightning and no thunder. And the bolts were hitting. It felt so strange. It wasn't as if his wandering habits were unknown to his family. They had been the cause of at least a couple of storms before. But he had always fought back or refused to take the accusations seriously. They couldn't prove it. After all, he had actually never been unfaithful to his wife. And when his little games had brought on static, he had always backed off, turned the game into innocent activity and eventually gotten out of it altogether. He had come to detect how much the family would tolerate, how far he could go, and within that boundary he had come to believe in his own innocence. Now, in cold blood, his sister was not merely questioning his innocence, she was naming his guilt. He could continue his activities, but not in her house and not with her friends, at least not with her co-operation.

For the first time, he felt his innocence drain from him. Where it went he didn't know. Perhaps under the coffee table. He sat on his chair accused, by himself as much as by his sister.

The old church was being dismembered, a limb at a time. An antique dealer had bought the stained glass windows and already one of them was resold and installed in the A-frame guest house of a local private resort. At least it would not be broken by vandals there. The altar rail was now part of someone's deck and the pews were in a local carpenter's work shed. They had never been very comfortable for sitting. The carpenter intended to dismantle them and use the wood for other purposes. Whatever else had been of value in the church had long disappeared. It was scattered in homes as far away as New England, some of it sold and resold so many times that its origins were no longer known.

The church building itself stood in the unmowed field, the gaping holes where the windows had been gave it a post-Halloween look, a look that was to be short-lived. The church was about to be torn down. A new Canadian Tire Store was scheduled to be built on the property within the year.

He felt sad and bitter about the demise of the old church. He had worshipped there as a child, and his ancestors had worshipped there for well over a hundred years before him. He sensed their collective disapproval and disappointment in their descendants. They were proud people, people who had left a legacy. Builders of a strong fishing industry, his ancestors were industrious people, hard-working, self-educated, dedicated and moral.

They had done well. From their small beginnings they had eventually produced clergy, lawyers, and doctors. One of their sons had become president of a university in Washington, another a chief justice in Florida. They had all gotten their start here, baptized from the waters of a well that was soon to be sealed underground forever by the asphalt parking lot of Canadian Tire.

The church had been ordinary enough during his growing-up days, the last days of the church's use. But he had always felt a sense of awe and reverence in the church, even when it had fallen into poorer times. He remembered his grandfather telling him of a time when men carrying beaver hats and gold knobbed canes walked up the aisle to fill the first four pews. The sanctuary lamp, a huge cascade of cut glass, had been brought here from Barcelona by a local sea captain. He wondered whose estate it ornamented now, and what the sea captain must think about this now, the same sea captain whose marble monument was lost in a sea of alders in the old cemetery.

He felt helpless about the present state of affairs. His own family had done well, and he had done well enough himself. But he couldn't look after everything alone. So many of the more prosperous members of his family had moved away. He had to admit to some resentment against them. While they spoke proudly of their heritage, they were not proud enough to make a contribution towards its continuation. His campaign for support of the church had elicited some response, but not nearly enough.

He felt bitterness toward the local people as well. There were many people who could have contributed towards the upkeep of the church. Their own ancestors were lying up in that field of alders too. Their lack of respect was difficult to accept. Perhaps they had dwindled to a number too small to maintain an actual parish with a resident priest, but there was enough money around to maintain the church and the cemetery. Besides, if people had been willing to help, much of the project could have been accomplished by means of donated labour. He felt ashamed of his community and of his family. And there was nothing he could do about it.

Down the road, an old widow also remembered the stories of the men with the beaver hats and the gold-knobbed canes. She remembered the stories without any nostalgia. Her grandfather had been a fisherman who had sat on a bench in the gallery because he had no money to buy a pew. The money for his fish had bought many beaver hats and had educated the university president in Washington. There were no alders on her grandfathers grave because she maintained it herself. And on his grave was the baptismal font from the old church, which she had put there years ago, as a birdbath. She kept it scrupulously clean and had already trained her grandson to care for it after she died.

"What man among you with a hundred sheep..."
(Luke 15:1-32)

Sometimes she wasn't even sure whether she loved her son. Certainly her life was less complicated, and her heart more peaceful when he was not around. She had never really felt loved by him.

From the beginning she had not been able to get close to him. While she had to push her other children off her lap like a mother bird pushing her young from the nest, he slipped off her lap long before having discovered its comfort. At first she had joked about it. She could afford to joke about it then . . . it was a relief to have at least one child so eager to look after himself. She said that he took after his father, an independent man who spent much of his time working or pursuing hobbies that were work-related and which took him away from family-centered activities. If she could accept this in her husband, she could certainly accept it in one of her children. She was not a greedy or possessive person, and had rather welcomed the fact that at least one of her children was more like his father than like herself.

But as he began to grow, she noticed that the likeness he bore to his father was only superficial. Her husband was independent and a loner, but he was far from being unaware of people around him. There was something of the good monk in her husband, the person who lives apart from the world but who still loves the world. If her husband did not share many activities with her and the children, she was always conscious of his love. They were together even when they were apart.

Not so the son who had been so quick to slip off her lap. Like his father he was interested in work, not so much because he liked it, but to get ahead. Where the father was independent because he didn't want to impose himself on anyone, the son was independent because he didn't trust anyone. Where the father liked to be alone in order to get in touch with himself, the son wanted to be alone in order to avoid other people's problems. Eventually she realized that her son was selfish. Later she realized that he was manipulative and would use other people to his own advantage.

He had to weave his web elsewhere . . . the family was too strong and too united to be manipulated. There had been many fights, of course, but he always lost them, and she was always left with the task of including him in a family where he didn't seem to belong. He, in turn, was never grateful for her efforts. Her efforts didn't succeed and he only rewarded whatever contributed to his own success.

He did well in the world outside his family. He was bright and excelled in athletics. He worked his way up in a large business firm and became its regional head of Public Relations. He had married well, to a woman with similar goals. Their children were still small, and it was too early to tell how they would turn out.

He maintained a curious relationship with his parents and siblings. None of them ever visited him because he could never make time for them, and they were just as happy, because he was difficult to be with. But he himself would come home for a week each year with the children. Curiously, he claimed that it was important for his children to know who they were and where they came from. At the same time, it was difficult to see how the children were learning anything about their roots. He monopolized the time at home lecturing his brothers and sisters on how they should improve themselves. It was a difficult week to get through for everyone. His wife did not accompany him. She said it gave her a break from him and the children.

This year his wife had enjoyed the break more than usual. He had returned to find out that she was making the break permanent. She was moving out. She was filing for a divorce. He could keep the children. All she wanted was half of what they owned.

He called his mother and asked if she could come and take charge of the household for a few months, until he could sort himself out and make other arrangements. He displayed no great emotion . . . he sounded neither angry nor grief-stricken. The only change his mother noted was that his speech was not as fast, that he had no explanations, and no solutions. He just stated the facts simply. She hoped that he might be in shock, that he might be stopped in his tracks, and that some good might come of this.

She packed to go. Her husband took a week off work to drive her and to spend a few days helping her get organized. On the two-day trip she shared her feelings with her husband. She was going because she didn't know what else to do. She had few hopes and no expectations. Her hopes centered on herself, that she might be capable of being a friend to this strange bird who had prematurely left her nest. She was glad that her husband would be with her the first days.

He had all he could do to stop himself from scolding his wife. The good life was right there for them. But it was passing them by and it was really her fault. He just had to make her see what she was doing.

He had retired at sixty-five, and for him it was a dream come true. For thirty years he had worked at the same job and wondered if he would ever see the end of it. He had. He felt doubly blessed, because he had savings and a good pension plan and was in remarkably good health. So was his wife. There are people who hate to leave their jobs behind. Not him. He was like a child with a new toy.

And in fact, he did have a new toy. He had bought himself a Winnebago. Completely furnished, it was actually nicer than their home. Much more convenient too, with no repairs to worry about. He couldn't wait to hit the road. For months now, he had pored over maps of every province in Canada and every state in the American union. They might not get to see them all, but they'd certainly make a stab at it. North in the summer, South in the winter. He imagined spending Christmas and the Summer Festival week at home, more or less to refuel and to visit the kids. Already he was writing post cards in his head.

The first summer was over now, and the farthest they had gotten was to Brierly Brook in Antigonish. Twice. The thought occurred to him that he had spent most of his life savings just to get to the Highland Games. Something was wrong. She was wrong. He couldn't get her to leave for more than four or five days at a time. There were always excuses. Her Aunt Sarah's funeral. Her niece's wedding. Their grandson's baptism. That was when he had hit the roof. Their grandson had been born in April, and should have been baptized then, if the priest hadn't been such a wimp and allowed them to wait until the summer so that they could have a barbecue. But then, what could you expect of the priests? They were the ones who started all this foolishness of waiting till babies were practically grown up before they baptized them.

He had gritted his teeth and waited till September when everybody got sensible and settled down, and all the relatives went home where they belonged. But now there were other reasons to stay home. She was into pickles and jellies. It wasn't her fault if they had such a wonderful crop of apples, and she certainly wasn't going to let them rot. He didn't buy that argument. She was only going to give all those pickles and jellies away anyhow. She kept hinting that she was going to miss the parish mission in October and was wondering who was going to look after her sister after she had her hip replaced in November.

He advanced his case. She was wearing herself out looking after other people. And little thanks she would get for it. Better for her to look after herself and him. This was what they had been looking forward to for years.

Correction, she said. She was looking after herself. She was not wearing herself out. She was doing what she enjoyed doing, what gave her life. When she was tired she didn't mind being tired. And when she was sad and troubled about someone, it was what she felt she ought to be. As for him, he didn't need looking after. He had always done okay for himself and could still do so. She reminded him that he was the one who had planned all this travelling. She was willing to do some with him too, but only as a treat now and then, and not as a way of life.

He knew she meant it and so he put most of his maps away. He kept the one of Newfoundland out, because she had a brother there who liked fishing. He figured they could manage that between the mission and the plastic hip.

In the meantime, he'd surprise her by joining the parish choir.

"And if your eyes should cause you to sin..."

(Mark 9:38-43,45, 47-48)

She knew she ought not to have looked into that room. She didn't even belong in the house. The only reason she was there was that her car had broken down and she had come to ask if she could use the phone.

The woman had been obliging. She not only allowed her to use the phone but had made her a cup of tea while she waited for the service man to come. After she had her tea, she asked to use the bathroom. And on the way from the bathroom she took the opportunity to look into one of the bedrooms. It was a stupid thing to do, and it was a serious breach of hospitality. But she could no more stop herself than she could stop herself from seeing whether the house was clean or not. She had an insatiable curiosity. And although she knew the woman who owned the house, she was not a friend of hers. She knew that she would never have another opportunity to get into the house again. This was her only chance. She could think of nothing else but to seize this golden opportunity to take a quick look around.

Her curiosity was rewarded far beyond what she had expected. She had expected to find antiques and dust. Instead she found evidence that the room was being occupied by a man. His clothes were not only strewn about, but there were some hanging in an open closet. She absorbed all of this within a few seconds, pulled the door back as she had found it and walked calmly down the stairs to find that the garage mechanic had arrived. She thanked the woman and left the house a guilty person.

She was not yet as guilty as she would be, because she could no more stop herself from telling than she could stop herself from seeing. She would not shout this out from the rooftops, for she was not a common gossip. No, she was a careful woman and not about to be caught explaining the embarrassment of how she had gotten her information. She would have to tell only one person. She would be careful to choose the right person, and she would be careful what she said. When the information became public, no one would know where it had come from.

Even as she enjoyed the thrill of her discovery, she wondered why she was doing this. She had nothing against the woman and no reason to do her harm. She normally didn't care all that much about who lived with whom. She considered herself a very modern woman in that way. What she couldn't stand was allowing people to have secrets. It bothered her to think that people could do things without her knowing. And exposing them was a way of punishing them for thinking they could keep things from her.

But people were on to her. They tortured her by holding back information that they gave to everyone else, so that she had to work harder to find out very ordinary things. Some even fed her false information to get her confused. What she didn't know as she gloated over this new story was what everybody else knew but had neglected to tell her. The woman whose phone she had used had taken her father in to live with her for the winter.

The dinner was ready, or at least it was ready in her mind. Stuffed turkey, pumpkin pie, the works. The silver was polished, the linen was starched, the arrangements of autumn leaves were all planned. It was the only feast for which she still polished silver and starched linen. She didn't even do it for Christmas.

Not that Christmas was less important to her than Thanksgiving. Christmas was, in fact, much more important to her, but it was a different kind of celebration. There was so much more to do to prepare for Christmas than polishing silver and starching linen. Christmas had enough activity without adding unnecessary demands. In her books, Christmas was about celebration not formality.

But at Thanksgiving she enjoyed the tasks involved in preparing for a formal dinner. The tasks served to slow her down, and she felt a need to be slowed down at this time of year. Decorating her house with autumn leaves got her out into the woods where she could not only see, but also touch, hear, and smell autumn. The linen was the only material thing of value that her mother had passed on to her. Treating it reverently helped her connect with all the traditions that had been passed on to her by her family. She didn't have to list them to herself . . . the images flowed before her eyes as the linen flowed between her fingers. The silver was the one extravagance she had allowed herself in later life . . . polishing it was polishing the memories of a life shared with children and friends, of hard work bringing satisfaction, and of joyful times in leaner years. The silver mirrored the richness of her soul.

If it took time to prepare this feast, it was time well spent. It was time to feel the fullness of harvest - the harvest of autumn and the harvest of life.

It was because of this that her disappointment was so deep when she learned that her two daughters and their families would not be home for Thanksgiving this year. Both daughters had to work on Sunday. This would leave them with only Thanksgiving Day off, and to come home would mean travelling back and forth on the same day, leaving them with barely enough time to sit down for dinner. Reluctantly they had to cancel.

If she had any grief herself, the grief would have to await the passing of her anger because she went quickly from disappointment to rage. She raged at greedy businessmen. She raged at spineless politicians. She raged at inconsiderate shoppers. She raged at materialistic daughters. She raged at a culture that had ceased to value her rituals, and she raged at a world that had chosen to live in a different time zone. Finally she raged at a world that had rejected her mother's linen and her own silver.

Her husband, who was both a practical man and a religious man, needed a plan to calm her rage. He had never seen her quite so angry, and he was worried. He saw a terrible weekend coming up, and he foresaw an icy winter beyond. He didn't like winter. What she needed, he said, was to act out her anger in an acceptable way. There was a precedent in the gospel parable of the king whose guests didn't show up. The king invited people off the streets to his banquet. Perhaps she could invite someone who lived alone, some poor people. Call the university and see if there were any foreign students with no place to go.

She was not impressed with his solution. She could not bring herself to admit to people that she was inviting them as a distant second choice, and she did not want to lie to them. Besides, she would probably still be very angry on Thanksgiving Day, and she didn't want anyone around if she was angry.

At the same time, though, there was something about the story that caught her attention. She was the one who treasured this feast and no one had the right to rob it from her. The king in the story was dead right about that one. She decided what she and her husband must do was to pull out all the stops in a feast day for two. She would share with others too but she would be a little more discreet than the king. And so she went out and bought a second turkey with all the trimmings, which she donated to the food bank. And then her own feast was on.

The silver had never shone quite so brightly and the linen had never felt quite so substantial. The wine had never tasted quite so fine, but then, she had gone to a specialty shop for it. She was feeling a wee bit tipsy when her daughters called, and she was able to truthfully tell them she missed them.

He smelled a trap. It was a familiar one, one that he had been caught in many times before. Sometimes he had gotten out of it without too much damage. Sometimes he had been badly hurt. A few times he had been able to see it coming and been able to disarm it before it sprang on him. He hoped this would be one of those few times.

He was being asked to play a game that others were playing but he had to play by different rules. What he was hearing was a little different from what was actually being said. He heard them say: "We expect you, because you are a sincere person, to give an honest answer to our question, but at the same time we are not sincere people ourselves and so our question does not have to be an honest one. Be warned . . . this is not an honest question, but you must treat it as an honest question."

It wasn't easy being a politician. He wondered what the question was going to be about. He wondered what issue he was going to have to take a personal moral stand on. He suspected that it would be either abortion or capital punishment, or perhaps gun control. The person asking the question represented a group attempt to draw him into the more popular controversial topics of the day. At times like this he wished he had never left the farm. He would probably end up saying that these questions were far too serious to be used as political football, and he would be accused of selling out. He longed to be in the woods cutting Christmas trees.

He had misread the group asking the question. The question turned out to be one of the environment versus the economy. He answered the question sincerely. Although it was a difficult question, it was not nearly so difficult as the ones he had imagined.

Two weeks later he was back on the family farm cutting Christmas trees. Not only had he misread the group asking the question, he had misread the voters reaction to his stand and they had voted him out of office. He ought not to have been surprised. He had never really belonged in Parliament in the first place. A lawyer or an economist would never have been outfoxed so easily. He was a farmer and he had spoken like a farmer.

Now the question was – could he live like a farmer? He enjoyed the outdoor work, he enjoyed the direct contact with nature, but he was also aware that he had grown soft. He liked the work, but he tired easily. He also discovered that he had as much office work to do here as in Ottawa. Here there were no paid secretaries, receptionists, accountants. There were no expense accounts.

He was also aware of political questions in a way that he had never been before. The use of herbicides, clear cutting, marketing boards - all were practical issues to him now, much more so than when he had been in politics. Free trade and the GST were now day-to-day realities.

He wondered where his head had been. He joined the local Woodlot Owners Association to discover that he was out of step and that his opinions were not very well respected. He had to learn what everyone else knew before he could be respected, and then he would have to come up with some original ideas of his own before he could even think of making a contribution. He was not invited to give talks anymore.

Being sincere was an expensive way to go. He found farming very hard and was not at all sure that it was what he wanted to do, but he didn't have much choice. His party had been defeated and there were no patronage appointments to be given out. He blushed with embarrassment now when he thought of all the speeches he had made in which he had boasted about how proud he was to be a farmer and how he understood the farmers' point of view. He was stuck now. He would have to learn to be a farmer. If he worked hard, if he ate a lot of crow, if he were lucky, perhaps he would make it. If he made it, he might even consider running for Parliament again.

In the meantime, Christmas meant selling Christmas trees, not decorating them.

He was not an honest man, and sometimes he despaired of ever being honest. It seemed to come so easy for so many people, and he wondered why it was so difficult for him. He wondered why he was even thinking about it. With all he had to think about, this seemed like a waste of time.

But for the moment he was caught. He was listening to a talk by an honest man, and it was bothering him, disturbing him, distracting him. He admired and envied the man, a man who had never taken the shortcuts that he had, a man who had suffered because he had not been willing to take shortcuts, a man whose calm and serenity he wanted for himself but doubted he would ever have. He wished he could stop the man from talking. He wished he had not come to this conference. At the same time he knew that he needed the business contacts that he would get at this conference. There was not even any hope of leaving early. He looked at his watch again.

His mind moved from the watch on his wrist to the first watch he had owned, at the age of ten. He had conned it off a kid in his class in return for some useless hockey cards. He had told his mother he got the money for the watch by selling magazines, and his mother had been very proud of him. It didn't feel like a total lie because he had actually sold the magazines. It was just that he used the magazine money to treat other classmates, impress them, and at the same time set them up for another con job. He tried to remember what had become of his first watch, but he couldn't. He knew that it had been used as leverage in some other deal.

His mind worked hard to remember the watch and what it looked like. He wanted to be able to see the face of the watch, but it eluded him, like so many faces since. It bothered him that he had done so well but that nothing he ever owned had any great meaning for him. It bothered him especially that he had no great respect for the countless people he had cheated in his life. But how could you respect people who were so easy to cheat. The odd person caught him, and that wasn't any better, bringing only embarrassment and disrespect for him. What bothered him the most were the people who weren't impressed with him, the people who just weren't interested in him, in what he had, or his ability to get it.

The present speaker was one such man, and now his mind returned from his reflections on his first watch to that man and what the man was saying. It wasn't what he was saying but the way he was saying it. He wanted to be like that man, to feel relaxed like that man, and not have to feel that he had to impress anyone. He wanted to be able to enjoy the conference without having to get anything material out of it. He didn't want to have to plan what he was going to do tomorrow. At this moment he would give away his first watch, and the watch he was wearing now (with its four diamonds) and all the watches he had worn in between, for that feeling.

The thought of letting his watches go seemed to quiet him a bit, and for a moment the watches and all the cheating they symbolized retreated from him. They did not quite go away. He could see them at a distance, but at a comfortable distance where they didn't seem to overwhelm his mind and overpower his thinking. He could actually hear what the man was saying now. He could almost feel what the man was feeling. It had a strange effect on him. He felt that he was suspended in mid-air, far from all the watches in the world and the people who were willing to be parted from them. He didn't dare raise his eyes to look at the man for fear that the spell would be broken. Instead he kept his eyes focused on a spot on the floor. It seemed to help his feet and his buttocks anchor him to the earth beneath him. His mind had no thoughts other than those he was hearing from the speaker.

The talk ended and he was able to raise his eyes and look around him. He felt rested, as if he had had a long sleep, and he felt light-hearted as if a heavy burden had been lifted from him. There followed a little break with a lot of chatter, and he was able to walk quietly out of the room without being observed.

"For to him all men are in fact alive..."
(Luke 20:27-28)

" *My corsage* is looking as wilted as I am," she said as she looked down at the arrangement of tiny yellow roses attached to her dress. It was four o'clock in the afternoon and the roses had put in a long day, and she had put in a long one hundred years. Today was her one hundredth birthday and her party was just beginning to wind down.

It had been a very successful day, from every point of view. She had gotten up early, not because she was nervous or because she felt any need to get herself ready, but simply because she was an early riser. Looking out of the window, she had been grateful that it was a fine day. She normally didn't go out after Thanksgiving, but she would be going to a round of activities today and had no wish to have a wintry November day needlessly initiate her last illness and demise. Otherwise, the backyard looked just the same as it had the day before, and more or less the same as it had for as long as she cared to remember. The sheds and the outhouse were gone and part of her history, but even her one hundredth birthday didn't bring them back clearly. She would have to work at that a bit, but for the moment her attention was with the day at hand.

The hairdresser had come in and worked her magic, and Susan had helped her dress. She had no children and her three husbands were gone almost as long as the sheds and the outhouse, so she lived with Susan, Susan's husband, and the three teenage boys, all of whom were very much family to her. Susan needed the pension money but wouldn't keep anyone just for money. Susan bought her a beautiful dress, and as she got into it she felt some of the beauty cling to her. She opted for jewellery but no makeup. She wanted to look her best, but she thought it only fair that everyone get a chance to see what a hundred year old face really looked like.

Off to church at 11 o'clock for a special mass of thanks-giving, then on to the parish hall for a lunch and open house. Cakes, addresses, telegrams and so many people—the works. No wonder the little yellow roses were beginning to nod. She had been smart not to wear make-up. By now it would be needing repair and she wasn't up to the challenge.

"How does it feel to be a hundred years old?" someone asked for what seemed like the hundredth time. "Not so good," she answered this time. "All my friends are gone." She was suddenly aware that there wasn't anyone who was over nineth in the room, but herself. A few stalwarts in their late eighties had come to envy and to hope, but they had not grown up with her and had not been close. All they shared was the anonymity of old age.

There wasn't a single person in the room who had been a part of the peaks and the valleys of her life. Her parents, her brothers and sisters, her school mates, her teachers, her neigh-bours, right down to the three husbands — all gone. Although the sheds and the outhouse were dim to her mind's eye, those faces were as clear as if they stood in front of her. They were certainly as clear as the faces that were now in front of her. She could see the age spots on the left side of her mother's face, she could see the shade of grey of her father's eyes, hear the bark of her first grade teacher, see the contours of each husband. Were they really gone, and were these other people really here?

She felt as if she had given the wrong answer to the young

man who had asked her what it felt like to be a hundred years old. She was straddling time and timelessness and it wasn't so bad at all. Her dead friends were very much alive to her, and so were all these people in the hall. Susan and her lovely boys, the women who organized the celebration, the priest who could share a joke with her like no priest had ever done when she was young, the young man asking her the question, who couldn't possibly understand, but who genuinely wanted to understand. The gift of her long life was to know both, to allow to mingle before her eyes the faces etched in her soul, the old friends, and the young faces in the room, celebrating life with her, venerating her. She allowed herself to mingle among them, to be young and venerated at the same time.

Thank God no one knew what was going on in her mind. They would think her daft. But they needn't know. In fact, another gift of old age was that young people generally allowed you to have your secrets.

By now the young man had moved on, and it was too late to correct him. Still, she appreciated his being here and hoped he would live long enough to find the answer for himself.

Every year she went through the same struggle — the struggle of Christmas shopping. It wasn't so much the actual shopping itself. She could deal with that easily enough if she could only settle on what attitude she wanted to take towards the shopping.

She would quickly settle the question of "why?" It was a spiritual matter for her. It had to do with what she believed in and how she saw herself in relationship to the world she lived in.

She believed that God was not an abstract concept or an old man living in the clouds. God lived in the world and that was worth celebrating. It was a high point at which she, who considered herself a religious person, could meet on common grounds with others, the religious ones and the non-religious ones. They could share common values of goodness, of beauty, of sharing, and of celebrating.

The custom of gift-giving was as old as the story of Christmas itself. Three kings had come bearing gifts to mark the wedding of heaven and earth. What was more, the gifts of the kings had been more extravagant than practical. Gold might have been considered currency, but teamed up with frankincense and myrrh, it wasn't quite what you would expect at a regular baby shower. The kings, who had much to share, had brought gifts to a family who possessed no material wealth. Perhaps it was just irony,but these kings must have felt the baby and his family didn't need a saddle for their donkey or a gift certificate for a week at the Bethlehem Holiday Inn. The gifts they brought were for someone the kings saw as having more than they had themselves.

She was pleased with this attitude towards gift-giving. It made gift-giving a gesture of homage and veneration, of recognizing the goodness and beauty of others and of acknowledging that openly. It opened up the sense of adoration in herself, made her feel like the kings or like the Virgin Mary's cousin Elizabeth, welcoming goodness and beauty into the world.

The problem was with the more practical part of the attitude–how to match the question "why?" with the question "who?" "what?" and "how much?" She looked at the Christmas list she had made up and sighed in despair. It wasn't finished yet and already she felt like handing it over to the minister of finance for editing. There were too many people on the list already, and it didn't include many of those she would really like to share with. It also felt too narrow, being made up of family, close friends, and professional acquaintances. She felt the need to break through those boundaries. The kings weren't friends or relatives of Joseph and Mary and were far from being professional acquaintances. There was no recognition of strangers in her list.

If there were problems with who was left out, there were also problems with some who were included. While she would gladly give a gold nugget to Uncle Howard if she could afford it, her own brother Wilfred would expect a dozen gold nuggets from her. He would be figuring out her salary and speculating on what she could afford to give him. He would probably exchange his necktie for a credit certificate if he thought he could get away with it. Her boys wanted guns and her girls wanted music she considered obscene. She had decided to give homemade mincemeat to her friends, knowing that one of them would want to improve on her recipe.

She made a silent prayer to the three kings although she doubted that they could be of help. They had not gotten their gold, frankincense, and myrrh at the mall, and it was unlikely that any of them had ever made mincemeat. This called for tough decisions. She started off by putting fifty dollars aside for "Loaves and Fishes." It would have to represent "the people who had everything." She knew what she wanted to give to her husband—that one was easy. He, in turn, would have to help her with the gifts for the children. She would need support in substituting something for guns and obscene music. Her husband would also have to look after his own family. She decided on mincemeat for Uncle Howard. If it was good enough for him, she could give it to anyone, including her brother Wilfred. He would protest that he didn't make pies and she would suggest that he learn.

Now facing the mall was a little easier. It was there that she found the Middle Eastern incense and decided to give some to everyone.

"The people stayed there watching..."
(Luke 23:35-43)

He was finding it difficult to think. He always found it difficult to think in a crowd. He liked to do his thinking alone. Away from crowds, away from radio and television, away from the confusing messages of the world.

The only messages that helped his thinking were the messages of nature, the call of birds when he was walking in the woods, the pounding of the surf when he was walking on the beach, or the whistle of the wind through the open window of his bedroom. It was in such spaces that he could allow thoughts to be born. After he had cradled the thoughts gently for some time, he would share them with his wife. She would acknowledge his thoughts, confirm them, tease them and challenge them. More birds, more surf, more wind, and then his thoughts were ready to stand the test of public scrutiny. That was why he seldom said anything in public. It took too long to get his thoughts together. By the time he was ready, the opportunity was usually past.

His head was pounding with noises now. The noises of angry voices. He didn't have the luxury of birds, surf and wind. Meanwhile, the moment was passing. He felt the pressure of the angry voices and he felt the pressure of the fifty or so silent people who were so taken up with following the angry voices that they were unable to find voices of their own.

He was sitting in the back row of the parish hall at the annual meeting of the Fishermen's Co-op, and the manager, sitting facing the crowd at the front of the hall, was getting crucified. There were calls for his immediate resignation, and judging from the temper of the meeting, the manager was not going to make it through the evening. The co-op was on the brink of collapse. It was probably going to collapse whether the manager stayed or went, but the mood was for punishing him personally rather than leaving its future in the hands of fate. The manager was immediately responsible for the situation the co-op was in, and it was important to get him before it was too late.

The manager was responsible for having taken some high risks. But then, it was only because of the risks that he had taken in his ten years as manager that the co-op had managed to survive at all. It had always been a shaky business and he had kept it afloat through risk, manoeuvring, and manipulation. The members had been okay as long as it worked. They were okay with risk. They were not okay with failure.

The manager was not responsible for the fact that he had to work with a weak board of directors and, more often than not, that he had to make up his own policy as he went along. He was not responsible for the recession, and he was not responsible for the lack of fish.

Lastly, the manager was not responsible for the greed of the members. For ten years now he had been trying to tell the members that they couldn't run a successful business without investing anything into it. They had never wanted to put any-thing into the business, and whenever there was a cent of profit, they wanted it to spend. They wanted jobs for their children, whether their children were good workers or not. And whenever they didn't get their own way, they sold their fish to the co-op's competitor, who trucked the fish away to be processed else-where.

They had not liked the manager's warnings. He was from away, and they didn't like being told what to do by a man from away. They especially didn't like the suggestion that they were greedy. He sounded as if he was better than they were. They had tolerated him for ten years because he had kept the plant open. Now the pent up grudges were coming out.

Accusation followed accusation. It was getting personal, and it was very doubtful that the manager would even try to defend himself. The few members of the board who believed in him were not going to speak for him either. They had faults of their own that would be brought up if they did. There were a number of people in the room who would have liked to believe this was all wrong, but who sat and waited. If the manager didn't defend himself, perhaps the accusers were right. Better to let him speak first.

From the back row of the hall, it was clear that the moment was passing, that it was almost past. Still no birds, surf or wind to clear a confused member's thoughts. But it was now or never. He stumbled to his feet and blurted it all out, calling upon the crowd to look at the manager's many accomplishments and at their own failure to work together in the past. Why not change that now, in this moment of crisis?

It was too late. The moment had passsed and his words were swept aside. Later he too would be swept aside. He sank back in his chair and thanked God he had gotten his little speech out at all. The co-op might be gone, but he was still intact.